# When Gucci Came First

## First
### *(True Tales of a Tramp)*

Written by: Kalico Jones

WildChild Press
Montclair, New Jersey 07042

©Copyright 1999 Mia Williamson.  All rights reserved.

No part of this publication may be reproduced, stored in a
retrieval system, or transmitted, in any form or by any means,
electronic, mechanical, photocopying, recording, or otherwise,
without the written prior permission of the author, except in cases
of short excerpts which may be used for reviews / articles.

IBSN: 0-9753082-0-3

Although this book is based on actual situations and
circumstance, its contents are fiction. Any resemblance to any
persons, places or things is purely coincidental and should be
regarded as such.

When Gucci Came First – Written By: Mia Williamson
Known by these works as
"Kalico Jones"

REPRINT 2008

Printed in USA

*Dear Reader:*

*I didn't write this book for fame or fortune. I wrote
this book in hopes that you will learn from my mistakes.
Although many circumstances in this book were built on
a foundation not of my own, I take full responsibility for
everything I have done, especially the things I have done
to myself.*

*Through many years of healing, I realize now I owe
myself an apology and so through this book, I say, "sorry"
to myself, in an effort to move on once and for all.*

*May God grant everything you ask for during your quiet
time with Him.*

*Respectfully,*
*K.J.*

To my daughter Ivana,
You were truly meant to be.

The contents of this book are fiction.

This book contains strong language and sexual content and is
not intended for minors.

# AND SO YOUR JOURNEY BEGINS

Last night, I was out with this guy "Q." He's a fellow PK (preacher's kid) at a bar in New Jersey. After having several drinks "Q" invited me back to his apartment. He said he had access to some good cocaine and since I hadn't seen him in a while I agreed to keep him company.

We walked two blocks from the bar to the apartment he shared with a friend who worked nights. Upon our arrival, "Q" told me that he had to go upstairs to get the "stuff" from a dealer who just happened to live in the building.

He returned 45 minutes later...

When "Q" re-entered the room. I immediately asked him how much my portion of the tab was. His response, "Nah Diamond, I got it." Now although my dear friend "Q" had offered to pay for our party favors, I didn't want him to think I owed him a "favor," so I gave him half the money he spent at his neighbor's house, $55.00.

I opened the little plastic baggie and scooped out some of an off-white, really close to yellow substance that was just passed off to me as cocaine and took a hit. Twice up each nostril. My nose froze immediately. I sucked my teeth and said, "There's too much cut on this shit...I can't sniff this crap, shit!" So pissed, having paid $55.00 for garbage, I grabbed a glass, filled it with Bacardi, dropped in two pieces of ice and decided to get drunk instead. But there was one problem, I started feeling high. I thought, "Damn, I hate being high off beat." I sat back on "Q's" bed, smoked a cigarette and waited for my high to come down.

30 minutes later...

My high was gone but my dear friend "Q" was just getting started. He was in the corner of his room (in front of the window, no less), rolling up a dollar bill like a straw. He snorted three lines of cocaine off the top of his dresser. I was flabbergasted and apparently that wasn't enough, because he then poured the little bit of cocaine left in the bag I had in a pipe and lit it!

Oh my goodness, he's a fucking CRACK HEAD!  I gotta get the fuck out of here quick.  I asked him to walk me back to the bar and he responded with, "Can I have a kiss?"

You should've seen the look on my face, utterly disgusted at this point (I just wasted $55.00 on bullshit, I can't get drunk and now he blows the little bit of high I had with this stupid ass question). "Sorry 'Q' but I don't do anything buzzed." He started laughing and took another hit of his dirty ass pipe.  To this day, I have never seen a person suck up smoke the way he did. I know the pipe LOOKED dirty, but was it clogged too?  Damn, he needs help.  He blew the smoke towards my face and replied in a Jamaican accent, "I respect that."

Yeah right...now you know his ass was lying.

"Can we please leave?"  I said, as I felt it necessary to ask his ass a SECOND time, to walk me back to the bar.  I put on my jacket and told him I was leaving.  He said he needed to change his shirt (that took fifteen minutes). He then tried on several suit jackets (another ten minutes) and finally at 1:15am, we were on our way out the door.  The bar was closed.

I walked home by myself in the freezing cold, clutching a torn piece of paper with his number on it.  I looked down at his number and thought, "I hope he doesn't expect to hear from me tomorrow." As a matter of fact, I hope he doesn't expect to hear from me ever again, fuckin' CRACK HEAD!

I know, I know,  How can I call him a crack head, right?

Listen...I have a weird perception of people who do cocaine. I guess it's because I don't consider myself an addict, and that whole crack pipe, smoking coke thing seems so offensively "fiendish" to me (if that's a word). I feel like this: if you sniff it, that's okay, a rich mans high and as long as you can afford it, you DO NOT HAVE A PROBLEM.  Now, if you SMOKE it, you're a fiend, period!

I guess my mindset on this is largely due to the fact that one of the TVs in my home was purchased from a pipe smoking fiend. It's a sick justification, I know, but as you will see, I've developed many sick justifications over the years.

When I'm not doing cocaine, I have a drink in my hand. I know it's substitution and you better not say shit to me about it, 'cause if you do, I'm gonna say, "At least I'm not getting high!" and I might tell you to go fuck yourself (depending on how many drinks I've had), so mind your fuckin'

business!

# THE FAMILY TREE

I can't recall my father living with my two brothers, our mom, and me. Sometimes I find myself trying really hard to remember, but I can't. As a matter of fact, the only time I can remember even seeing my father outside from an occasional Glen Island family cookout was:

1.  On the street. You see hard times never effected out father because he never really took care of any of his children (thirteen and counting), so he could afford to buy the cars he would be driving PAST us in because he was too afraid that if he stopped, we would ask him for money. BASTARD!

    or...
2.  When we did something that required a beating. That's right, I said beating. And it wasn't that our mother couldn't get her point across if she had to, but I guess she just got tired of being the one to handle that aspect of parenthood all the time.

**I used to compare my father to that verse from Psalms; you know the one... "Do not seek council from false prophets" (he's a minister now), until I got to know him, and you know what? He's not bad after all. As a matter of fact, he's GREAT! And we currently have a wonderful relationship; I think I'm his favorite! (Just joking, he loves us all the same).**

**My mother**
Now how does the fruit criticize the tree? My mother and I have a love / hate relationship. If we're on the phone and I piss her off, she'll hang up on me. If she pisses me off, I'll hang up on her.

One day (and this is just to give you an example of how mom gets down), she called me and we started to argue...well, I had made up my mind that SHE was NOT going to hang up on me, so I hung up on her first. Why did I do that? Don't you know home girl called me back, this time cursing and yelling louder than before, threatening to SEE ME IN THE STREET! I quickly apologized and tried to joke my way out of the confrontation she so eloquently promised me. It didn't work.

I remember another time I was mouthing off to her and she said, "there will be a police car and an ambulance outside of this house if you don't shut up and I'm getting in the police car!" Can you believe that shit? My own mother, a gangster – she's a very strong woman, she's endured a lot...I just wish she would socialize with others more.

## My brother Joey

AKA Big Mutha Fuckin' Joe as he likes to be called. I heard he got that name from some girls, I don't know, but little does HE know, he ain't getting shit from me for Christmas now that he has a son. I'm even thinking about cutting out his birthday gifts too. And DON'T even THINK about saying I'm wrong. Hell, that's what happens when your child is born the DAY AFTER your birthday. My brother Joey is crazy. Here's an example: A few years back, a very close friend of our family died. After the funeral everybody was at the house of the deceased eating and drinking, when someone asked for a drink. And out of all the people in the house to be thirsty, why did it have to be the very person my brother didn't like and can't stand to this day? Of course, he would be more than happy to fulfill her request for what I think was Gin and soda. Well...and keep in mind this is a true story...he gave Rhonda the drink, as she requested and stepped back into the kitchen and watched her through the window in the hall.

Now when I say he watched her, I'm not trying to say he glanced at her to see if she was enjoying her drink, I'm saying he was especially attentive. Even inquisitive, asking her several times how her drink tasted. Nice of him, maybe to someone who didn't know him, but I'm his sister and I KNEW something was going on.

I decided to keep my mouth shut and let the situation unfold.

My suspicions were confirmed when I noticed my brother looking at Rhonda's throat, watching it carefully as though he was analyzing her every swallow. It was as if he could see inside her neck, through her skin and all.

My heart raced as I thought to myself, "I hope he didn't poison this bitch." What did he do to her drink?

# When Gucci Came First

Well just as Rhonda took her final swallow, a chilling smirk came across my brother's face and then it finally hit me. I looked up at him and whispered, "You spit in it didn't you?" He turned and replied, "Yup." He poured it, spit in it, and watched her drink it as if him spitting in it wasn't satisfying enough. He's crazy, I tell you, just crazy.

Growing up, Joey and I never really had any major beefs. The only thing I hold against him is the fact that he never went after his dream to become a professional basketball player. He didn't even make a serious attempt, and he's good. And I'm not talking about the good your mother tells you you are because you're her child.
**My brother Charles…The "Baby"of the bunch.**

But don't call him that to his face or he'll go the fuck off.

One day I introduced him as my "little" brother to a co-worker and my goodness, you would have thought I stole his chicken… 'cause he turned to me and yelled, "Don't call me your fuckin' little brother, I hate that shit!"

Well, this may not mean anything to you, the cursing and all, and it probably shouldn't, but picture this coming out of the mouth of someone who rarely uses the word damn and THAT'S IN THE BIBLE. I was shocked, but also relieved. At least he wasn't the nerd we thought he was, "Whew, what a relief!"

My brother Charles… he's going to be a lawyer one-day.

The relationship my brothers and me have is great. Now don't get me wrong, we've had our share of fights growing up. Okay, we've had a lot of fights growing up, but its not like anyone ever had to stay in the hospital overnight or anything like that.

We're truly connected my brothers and me. We often say we have ESP, but only when it comes to each other. Kind of like "select ESP." Our relationship is so strong that I can think of my brothers then my phone will ring and it would be the brother I was thinking of on the line. Coincidence? I thought so too, so I tried it over and over. Still, the brother I was thinking of would call. I have to admit sometimes the wrong brother has called, but I'm sure

you get a clear picture of our closeness.

# A CHILD IN THE HOOD

I never thought my childhood was a "sunny" experience, for me growing up one of three kids living in a single parent household in the projects of Mt. Vernon.  But now when I look back, I see my childhood was better than the average childhood of a kid living in a single parent household with two other siblings in a two-bedroom apartment in the projects of Mt. Vernon.

"I'm never going to live in Mt. Vernon when I grow up!" I would tell my brothers after looking out of our ninth floor apartment window, from which you could see the lights of New York City on a clear night.

It's that very view of New York City, on a clear night, combined with our mother letting us take the number two train all the way from 241st Street and White Plains Road in the Bronx (by ourselves), to East 116th Street to our Aunt Cheryl's house, that made me realize, there WAS life outside of Mt. Vernon.

Those train rides to visit our family (my mother is originally from Harlem) exposed me and my brothers to "real life."

**SIDE TRACKED FOR A MINUTE...**

**Tuesday, 7:20A.M. Hot 97FM "Roll Call"**

"What's up y'all? Whatcha gotta say? Who's on the phone with Ed, Lisa and Dre?"
"It's Kalico, the one who everybody knows, brown skin, nice body, short hair cut and pigeon toes."
"Well that sounds good, and that may be, but where ya calling from, tell us what city?"

"Heavy Diddly Diddly Dee-Ville is where I'm from, Big up, Big up to Mt. Vernon."

# When Gucci Came First

Yeah, I think I'm cute. Yeah, I know I'm attractive. A lot of people will agree with me, a few women won't...fuck 'em! I only got one life to live and if any of this "the end of the world is near" shit is true, we may not have too much time left, so I'm doing whatever the fuck I want.

# LET ME TELL YOU A LITTLE BIT ABOUT MYSELF

One good thing about me is that I rarely lie.  My philosophy on lying is simple (and this is coming from a reformed habitual liar): It makes no sense to lie because once you lie, you have to keep lying and lying and lying and before you know it, you're on some real fairy tale shit, fully equipped with Alice and the entire Wonderland Crew.  And then down the road, when asked, you won't be able to get that shit to flow right.  So why even bother?  And besides, what is going to happen to you that is so bad that you have to lie in the first place?  NOTHING!

I'm also a giver.  I'll give my time, my money, whatever I have to help someone.  Now don't get me wrong, I'm not parting with all my shit, but I will give what I can.

The last great thing about me is that I'm creative.  I think its because I fantasize a lot.  My imagination doesn't run away with me, it takes a plane!  But don't worry, it's not like I'm pretending to be a movie star, although I have imagined myself on the big screen once or twice.  Okay, okay you got me, THREE TIMES...Damn!

**School days**

Grimes Center for Creative Education, my elementary school.  A school with a curriculum designed to stimulate creativity was located in the dead ass Boone docks...way on the "other" side of town.  Not a nigga in the area, unless they attended the school, worked at the school or cleaned those big ass houses that surrounded the school.  Funny, but sadly true.

Grimes was a very good school and I tried to take advantage of everything it had to offer a "Southside" kid like me. And believe it or not, I held my own. You name it, my ass was in it: Science fairs, jazz class, tap, ballet, photography and drama. "Hey Mrs. Reid, now I see where all those chorus lessons paid off...in the shower, 'cause I still can't sing!" ha ha ha.

# When Gucci Came First

A.B. Davis Middle School was the next stop for me and I was kind of popular, but only because I was from the projects and the project kids were considered to be "hard." I did pretty well in seventh grade, especially in English. Maybe it was because I had the opportunity to use my imagination through writing essays, or maybe it was because I had a GORGEOUS teacher. Maybe both.

Nichols...eighth grade. I don't know why this is, but I only have one memory of 8th grade. It was when the school did a rendition of the then popular television show "Puttin' on the Hits" – You remember the show...the one you had to lip-sync to a popular song. Randy O'Neal and me performed "I feel for you" by Chaka Kahn. We came in second place. Everyone said we should have won first place. You should've seen me, I had on my mother's black dress with silver sequins, and one of my grandmother's wigs. Every time I hear that song, I smile. I wonder if Randy remembers that.

Mt. Vernon High School (my next stop) was no walk in the park. There's only one high school in Mt. Vernon so being popular wasn't based on where you lived like 7th and 8th grade. You see HORMONES were in effect and boys were looking at tits and ass and here I was...skinny, pigeon-toed and STILL a virgin! Yeah, I had my group of friends and a few boys liked me, but I was so crazy about Walter Greene. I even put letters in his locker! It was difficult trying to be popular, trying to keep up with the older girls and trying to be cute, so I gave up. And as soon as I did...it happened.

My family and I moved to Yonkers. Now for those of you who don't know where Yonkers is...GOOD, you don't need to know (just joking). Yonkers is so close to Mt. Vernon (the next town over), you can actually walk there. I call Yonkers, Mt. Vernon's cousin.

Yonkers, NY 10701 equated to instant popularity, but only because I was the new piece of pussy on the block. Niggas flocked to me like they had bets on who would fuck me first, but I was still a virgin, although I didn't act like it. And since I know some of you reading this book know me personally -.I'm going to say it again - I WAS STILL A VIRGIN (10th grade, 11th grade). I say this twice because of you people that will swear you know me well enough to say I wasn't and for this guy let's just call him Mr. First, from Mt. Vernon, who will say he was the first person to have sex with me in the Fall of 1986, but he is LYING! And since this is the truth, the whole truth and nothing but the truth, for the record, I will tell you how it went down and let you be the judge, okay?

# When Gucci Came First

## THE CIRCUMSTANCES

After moving to Yonkers, I continued to travel back and forth between Mt. Vernon and Yonkers everyday. Yes I was kind of popular, but only with the boys, so I would go to Mt. Vernon to hang out with old friends until I was able to meet new girls who lived in Yonkers to replace them. FYI...I wasn't successful.

Anyway, back to Mr. First...

## THE SET UP

After my first day of classes at my new high school, Lincoln High, I went to Mt. Vernon. I ran into two of my friends who were deeply involved in a conversation about sex. I tried to join in, but when I revealed to them that I was still a virgin they felt I didn't have anything to contribute to the conversation, so they changed the subject. They started asking me about my new school and if I had made any new friends. Mid conversation, this guy, Mr. First, rode past us on his motor bike. I really had a thing for this guy and I guess he liked me too, who really knew, but anyway my two friends walked over to Mr. First. I stayed behind and waited for them to return. When they got back, one of them said to me, "You should do it with him." The other one added, "It feels good, it doesn't hurt." And after what seemed like hours of convincing, I agreed.

## THE BIG EVENT

Well, Mr. First took me to his Uncle's apartment on West 4th Street and attempted to get his dingaling in me. Poking, rubbing, using his fingers, I was scared. How did I allow these bitches to talk me into some shit like this? I was actually giving up my virginity to someone based on the thoughts and opinions of two girls I personally thought were dumb. Lucky for me, his Uncle came home and we had to leave. As Mr. First walked me to the number seven bus stop, by what was then Waldbaums, he told me to "come back tomorrow" and we would "try with Vaseline."

## WHAT WOULD YOU CALL THAT?

## My FIRST or FIRST ATTEMPT?

Just what I thought, my first ATTEMPT. I didn't go back to Mt. Vernon

# When Gucci Came First

for several months.

Two and a half years after that, I lost my virginity to Cool T, a big Willie motherfucker from my new hometown.  He and his brothers had all the cars, money and bitches a nigga could only wish for. Stanley Place in Yonkers... that block would be lined with exotic vehicles from one corner to the next, and I'm not talking about the short side of the block, I'm talking about from corner to corner, THE LONG WAY! I would look out my window in full amazement of the shit they had parked out there; assorted BMWs, Saabs, Motorcycles, Milanos. Yeah, those brothers knew how to play BIG!

Cool T, a nigga that if you had his hands, you would cut yours off and I was in love.  I remember telling him that all the time and he would look at me and laugh.  "You're too young to know what love is," he'd say. I still insist I was in love.

# BEING THE NEW PIECE OF ASS
# IN THE NEIGHBORHOOD

Was beginning to wear me down.  I had to always look good, while trying NOT to make too many girls mad at me at the same time.  Trying not to make females mad at me was hard, especially since I had someone looking out for me, someone who was like a big sister.

Jaimie was the flyest girl in Mt. Vernon. She was light-skinned with a big ass and pretty smile.  Good-looking girl with a shape that was out of this world! Small waist, nice legs… she was a "10" (just ask anyone) and she knew it too, 'cause everything she wore complimented her figure. When Jaimie walked down the block, men would stop right where they were, just stop.  They could be with their girlfriends and everything! Jaimie had it going on and I looked up to her and Bean.

I would braid Jaimie's hair and she would give me clothes, shoes, sneakers, jewelry, and all types of expensive things.  She even gave me my **FIRST GUCCI BAG.**

I don't know why Jaimie adopted me on some ol' little sister shit, but she did and I was grateful.  She made sure I was one of the flyest girls in the school and because of her, that popularity thing was easy.  The guys liked me, the girls loathed me, but everyone wanted to be my friend. And by month three of attending my new school, I had a bunch of female friends.

Too bad none of those friendships lasted, except for my friendship with Marilyn Stevenson.  She died in a car accident in 1987 or 1988. At any rate, I was devastated.  I still feel the loss sometimes, seeing her all dolled up in that peach dress in a casket. Devastating, I tell you.  Just ask anyone I've ever been in a car with how her death affected me.  I'm always like, "don't drive fast," "slow down," "watch out for that car."  Sometimes I'm even like, "fuck it, just let me out." My current boyfriend says I'm a backseat driver and is forever calling me paranoid, but it's because of her tragedy that I don't

# When Gucci Came First

accept rides from people I don't know personally and I don't allow anyone to drive reckless, over the speed limit or under the influence of drugs or alcohol, with me in the car. I hope you don't either.

I'm aware of the saying, "friends don't let friends drink and drive," but sometimes you can't stop people from doing what they want and exercising their right to do what they very well please – no matter how stupid. Therefore, I have NO PROBLEM with saying this: "If you cannot stop the one you're with from driving under the influence, STOP YOURSELF from getting in the car! There's only one you...save yourself."

Marilyn Renee Stevenson was in the backseat of the vehicle and STILL died. She was the only one do did.


Sorry, I went off the road a bit, but I had to get that off my chest.

Anyway, Lincoln High School was turning out to be a not so good experience for me once people found out I was from Mt. Vernon. I began to encounter bullshit. Me, Stephanie, and Larki (R.I.P.) were all from Mt. Vernon and although my brother Joey attended the same school, he never had any major problems. My mother said it was because Joey minded his business and didn't have a nasty attitude like me. And she was right, 'cause Joey never got into much trouble, but me...EVERY chance I got, my ass was in something. I stayed fighting and because I didn't loose; I thought I was "bad."
I remember one time me and Larki were sitting outside of Mr. Hodus' office (school principal), about the get in trouble, when we looked down and noticed that we both had on Gucci footwear. He had a the moccasins, and I had on the sneakers; we got a kick out of that. We may have been in trouble, but we sure looked good!

At this time, Heavy D was big in the rap game and since I was from Mt. Vernon, I was particularly proud of him. I was so proud of him that I'm not even going to tell you what I did with a member of his crew, let's just say, I'm "cool peeps" with a close associate (wink...wink). Hey, don't get mad at me for not saying who and what - this man is married with children and shouting him out could start a conflict in his home. DAMN! Have you no shame? (ha ha ha).

I remember walking the halls of Lincoln High School singing Heavy's hit single, "Mr. Big Stuff." I only did that because I knew some people didn't like me because I was from Mt. Vernon, and being the person I was, and still am (sort of, kind of) to this day, I would sing it LOUD and proud. Loud and proud until one day someone yelled, "We don't like Heavy D here!" Could you believe that? How could someone NOT like Heavy D? I quickly turned around to see who said that and everyone's back was turned. So you know me, I started singing again…"I'm rough and tough and all that stuff, I make ya dance and prance, 'til ya huff and puff, there's just no way you can get enough…" and again someone yelled out, "We don't like Heavy D, here!" and once again, I turned around and…

**FELL IN LOVE!**

They called him "Box." He had on a red Polo jacket and was popping his gum. I thought he was so cute and after several days of staring at him and getting Carrie to give him messages from me, I went over and made conversation.

"Nice jacket, where did you get it?"

I can't recall what he said, I think it was NBO or was it BFO… well it was something like that. At any rate, from that conversation, we started seeing each other. "Box" and I would spend time together after school. He hung out in School Street projects with Chucky Walker and Mike Lou. We would take long walks, hold hands, and kiss. I really liked Box and everyone knew it.

He and I quietly dated for a while, but he had to break up with me because his crazy ass ex-girlfriend and her friends wanted to beat me up.

"Box…" It wasn't until I moved out of Yonkers, years later, that we slept together. NO COMMENT.

# LINCOLN HIGH SCHOOL
# PRINCIPAL'S OFFICE

That day in Mr. Hodus' office ended up being a very bad day for me. Turns out I was called to the office because of chronic class cutting, and overall absenteeism. Mr. Hodus was now requesting a meeting with my mother. I tried to talk him out of it, but when I couldn't identify my first period teacher, that spoke for itself.

I was excused for the remainder of the day.

Shit! How am I going to tell my mother that I may be getting kicked out of school? How do you explain this kind of shit to a crazy person? And don't be looking like, how can I call my mother crazy, shit, she's crazy! And we all knew it (me, my brothers, and few former neighbors). I think it had something to do with her childhood or maybe it had something to do with her marrying our father and having three kids before she really had the chance to grow up. Maybe it was all these things, or maybe none, but whatever the cause, the fact remained the same...SHE WAS CRAZY!

As I walked out the school pondering thoughts of getting on the next bus headed to Philadelphia to join my sister Shantel, and her mom Shirley (anything to keep my mother from fuckin' me up at this point), I noticed a guy wearing a pair of work boots with a neck full of jewelry.

I heard him ask someone to introduce us.

His name was Kenny and he smelled like a jar of Egyptian Musk, his "signature" smell. He was funny, and boy oh boy was he generous. I didn't even have to break him in. He would just give me money and jewelry. He took me places and I was HIS new girlfriend. There was only one thing wrong with him, he had a bunch of kids, he was older than me and he was a drug dealer. I guess that could be three things (depending on how you view it).

Even though Kenny sold drugs, he kept a job at Shop Rite or Path Mark (can't remember which one), so he had more money than someone who just did one or the other.  I liked Kenny and he liked me.  By the way, did I mention he drove?  A Suzuki Samurai!  I couldn't ask for a better boyfriend, at that time in my life.  I was walking around looking like Mr. T's wife (I had on so much jewelry). Between Jaimie giving me clothes and Kenny giving me money, I was doing great! But I never slept with him and it wasn't until I went to his house for a visit months into our relationship that he EVEN TRIED to have sex with me. And come to think of it, it wasn't until that day at Kenny's house that I ever experimented with drugs.

When I arrived at Kenny's house, he had company. His friend Steve from down the block on Warburton was there working on some new music for a demo tape.  You see, Kenny was into music just as much as he was into selling drugs, making babies and working at Shop Rite or Path Mark, or whatever food store it was.

I was sitting on Kenny's bed when he pulled out a piece of foil and unfolded it.  There was cocaine inside.

"Here, take some, " he said. I tried to explained that I didn't do drugs, and that I did not wish to try it, but just like that day I let my childhood friends talk me into having sex before I was ready, I let Kenny convince me into trying cocaine. I stood up, took a few sniffs, and then sat in the broken chair next to his bed.

All of a sudden, my heart started beating fast, and then faster and then faster. Damn! I'm thinking… "Why did I do this to myself?  I should have just said no."  I was high as a kite, and Kenny knew it.

He asked Steve to leave.

I knew I was in trouble then.

I tried to get Steve to stay, but Kenny insisted he leave. As Steve closed the door behind him on his way out, Kenny pulled me up out of the chair by my shirt and started rapping.  Yes, you heard me correctly, his ass started FREE-STYLING off the top of his head, some shit like, "Yo Kalico, I really wanna see ya" as he tried to feel my tits.  When I resisted, he got forceful.  I decided not to excite him by yelling, so I kept calm and asked him to unlock the bedroom door.

# When Gucci Came First

He wouldn't.

All he did was talk about all the money and jewelry he'd given me and how I wouldn't give him what he felt I now owed him because of those gifts... PUSSY!

My high had begun to develop into full-blown fear, as I was now scared for my safety.  Here I was in a locked room, with a man too big for me to fight off, and if I did get out, how was I going to get home? I had no money AND I lived ALL THE WAY on the Southwest end of Yonkers. It was dark and absolutely too late for me to even think about walking, but that was exactly how Kenny decided I would have to get home if I refused to fuck him.

Walking home late at night, by myself and high was a small price to pay for freedom.

Freedom of a situation I brought on myself.

Having now made the decision that I would rather walk than to give up some pussy, I begged Kenny to let me out of his house.  When he finally agreed, I was missing two buttons on my shirt and my hair was a mess.  I quietly left the premises and started to pray.

"God, I know I did something wrong tonight, but if you please just get me home safe I promise I will try really hard to be more careful with my decision making from here on out, thanks...Amen."

About a half block into my "freedom walk" I saw Kenny's friend Steve, the one who was over making a demo tape earlier that night.  I told him what transpired between me and his friend. Steve flagged down a cab and paid for my ride home.  I promised to pay him back when I could, and quickly got my broke, high, scared, missing two buttons on my shirt, messy hair ass in the taxi.  I could hear Kenny's voice in the background.  He was yelling something, but I never turned around.

The next day Kenny was at my house, trying to reconcile.  Not learning my lesson, I continued to take things from him after that episode at his house, but I never went back there and I never went anywhere with him if I didn't have a friend to take with me.

I eventually moved on.

Oh...and I never fucked him.

It wasn't until years after that incident at Kenny's house that I experimented with drugs again.
A few years ago, I asked someone how Kenny was doing. They told me he was out of jail and doing fine – I believe he may own a business.

Good for him!

Dating Kenny made it bad for me. By this time, I was dubbed a "gold digger" and unfortunately haven't quite lived that down to this day. People from Mt. Vernon were saying I was trying to be like Jaimie, but no one knew exactly HOW she stayed so fly. All they knew was that she didn't have a job. I didn't have a job either, but I was in school and I had Jaimie – she was my secret weapon. And until about age 22, she played a major role in my life.

I guess I DID want to be like her, but be myself too. I would never date anyone who couldn't help me. I didn't give a damn about how they looked. As a matter of fact, I tried to stay away from the nice looking guys. I dated ugly boys, ugly teenagers, and ugly men. Ugly, ugly, ugly...but they all had one thing in common...MONEY AND ME, I guess that's two things, huh?

"But she's a smart girl," I heard my mother say through the door of the

# SCHOOL PRINCIPAL VS. MY MOTHER?

Principal's office at Lincoln High School, after being told I was being kicked out and placed into P.S. 31. P.S. 31, an alternative high school for kids with behavioral problems and adults who wanted to continue their education.

"You've seen her test scores," my mother continued, as she pleaded with Mr. Hodus to reconsider his decision.

"Mrs. Jones, your daughter has been involved in several incidents here at the school, and although I will agree Kalico is an exceptionally bright young lady, she barely attends her classes, and when she does, I'm told she is easily distracted" My now former principal explained his reasons for my expulsion.

I was called into the office and told to sit down. My mother took a deep breath and asked me what my problem was. I replied, "they don't like me cause I'm from Mt. Vernon."

Next thing I knew...WHAM!

My mother slapped me! I felt a slight wetness in my mouth. Was my mouth bleeding? I placed my hands over my lips to catch the blood. I TOLD Y'ALL SHE WAS CRAZY... she done (Ebonics) slapped blood out of my gums right in front of the fuckin' principal and he ain't say shit!

Bill, my mother's boyfriend at the time, who was in attendance (THANK GOD!), put his arms around my mother, who looked as though she wanted to cry, and we left the school.

Damn, its gonna be a long ride home.

"No more sneakers, no more jewelry, clothes, nothing...Do you think being cute is more important than going to school?"

# When Gucci Came First

I answered, "No Mommy."

WHAM! She slapped me again.  This time I felt my top lip swell.

"Don't talk back to me!" my mother yelled

I kept my mouth shut for the rest of the afternoon.

I started P.S. 31 the following week.

Have Jackhammer will travel.  I was taking Yonkers by storm and WAS NOT giving up the ass.  I was just getting what I could get, then jet.  So much to the point that my friends, Darlene and Charlene (twins), nicknamed me "Jetta."

Darlene and Charlene...my fuckin' peeps to this day.  I would go to Mt. Vernon and get drunk and high and have to sleep over their house 'cause I couldn't make it home.  And each time I got drunk and high I would try to kick it to this guy. Let's just call him Mr. M3 BMW of Mt. Vernon.

Now, I'm gonna tell y'all a story...and you know what?  Its going to be an important lesson in it, so PAY ATTENTION!

# MR. M3 BMW

Mr. M3 BMW of Mt. Vernon was cute, had a nice body (from what I could see), and he drove a BMW. I heard the car was a "gift" from a female friend. At any rate, Mr. M3 BMW of Mt. Vernon would come over to the twins' house to hang out and each time he was there, and after I had a few drinks, I would tell him how good he looked and try to invite him over to my house. He would always turn down my invitation.

Now remember I wasn't accustomed to anyone turning me down, so again one night after I consumed one too many drinks, I invited Mr. M3 BMW of Mt. Vernon to my house, and again he turned me down. His response to me this time was, "No, I don't want no drunk pussy, you stay drunk all the time...No I'm not fucking you, you're alright, but I don't want to fuck you, stop asking me that shit!" He said it, right to my face, right in front of everybody. I couldn't believe it.

Needless to say, I never approached him in that manner again, drunk, sober or indifferent. As a matter of fact, I tried not to drink in front of Mr. M3 BMW again. If I was in the Twins' house drinking and he came in, I would stop. But that's not the lesson.

A few months after he yelled at me, I got a call from my neighbor Harry. He told me that Mr. M3 BMW of Mt. Vernon was in the hospital. There were rumors that Mr. M3 BMW of Mt. Vernon had Hepatitis and I believe T.B., but both were untrue, 'cause Mr. M3 BMW had AIDS.
I called the hospital.

Ring... Ring... Ring...

"Hello" (It was Mr. M3 BMW of Mt. Vernon) his voice was faint and kind of high pitched.
"Hey, its Kalico, how ya feeling?"
"Fucked up."

# When Gucci Came First

I couldn't believe he cursed!  His ass should've been praying. And I'm not trying to be funny, nor am I making a joke about death, dying or disease, so DONT EVEN THINK ABOUT WRITING MY ASS A LETTER ON THIS! I'm just saying that since he was getting ready to see Martin Luther King, I thought
his choice of words could've...no, SHOULD'VE been different.

But this was my friend. In fact, since he didn't fuck me, he was my BEST friend.  I felt the need to do something to show him my gratitude for turning down all my advances.

"Do you need me to bring you anything?" I asked.
"No"
I took a deep breath and said, "You listening..."
"Yeah" He replied, this time his voice more faint than when the conversation began.
I exhaled and said, "Thanks."

I hung up the phone and prayed. Under the circumstances, I thought it would be best for me not to visit him.

Mr. M3 BMW died a few days later.
The weeks that followed were filled with rumors of who had what, who fucked who, and so forth.  Me, I don't think I was ever too involved in that rumor, but hey...you never know.

Gossip to me is simple:

**"Nobodies talking about nothing to other nobodies!"**

And if I WAS part of that "who fucked Mr. M3 BMW of Mt. Vernon" rumor...I COULD CARE LESS!

Just find a moral in that story and remember that MERCY is GOD not allowing something to happen to you that your ass probably deserves.

Okay, so for about a year after that whole Mr. M3 BMW of Mt. Vernon dying thing, I would continue to pop in and out of Mt. Vernon.  You see, I had found me someone else to "like" and since he was the local "number man," I would hang out around the local number "joint" and wait for my new

# When Gucci Came First

interest, Mr. Older Man to show up.

# I'M IN LOVE WITH A MAN
## NEARLY TWICE MY AGE

Mr. Older Man gave me money, drove me home after nights of me hanging out with the Twins and he would even let me give him kisses once in a while, but he refused to sleep with me.

I'm thinking... "Damn, not two niggas in a row" and "is he trying to protect me from something as well?"

I know he wanted to sleep with me, I saw the way he looked at me whenever I was around. Watching me walk, commenting on my "sweet" kisses, etc. but he would not have sex with me. He tried to say it was because he and my uncle were friends, then he claimed I was "too skinny" and continued to ignore my advances. As a matter of fact, his actual words were, "You're ass ain't big enough!"

I couldn't believe he said that, as I have always kept a decent shape and quite frankly thought my ass was just fine. I begged a mutual friend, let's refer to him as "Woo," to ask Mr. Older Man to take me out on a date. I can't tell you if our mutual friend ever did that for me. All I can tell you is that Mr. Older Man ignored me until I brought my friend, Joanne to Mt. Vernon to "hook up" with Woo.

Woo and Joanne hit it off immediately and I was glad for them, but I was thinking of myself the entire time they were seeing each other. I hoped that one day, we could ALL double date. Me with Mr. Older Man and Joanne with Woo. After weeks of my continued sexual advances and Woo's nagging, Mr. Older Man asked me out on an "official" date. We were going to City Island for dinner in his convertible Corvette.

Anyway, as we get to the turn off point where the restaurant strip was located and Mr. Older Man said, "That's the exit we would have taken if we were going to get something to eat." I looked at him and asked where we were headed. His response, "To a place where I can give you what you want."

# When Gucci Came First

And that's just what he did.  I enjoyed myself too, until he made a call and passed the phone to me.  It was my friend Joanne, she and Woo were in the next room (I knew that voice sounded familiar as we could hear screaming through the wall). Anyway so I'm on the phone with Joanne chatting and then came the ultimate...

Mr. Older Man asked if we could "switch."

Time to go. I said nothing the whole way home.  I was completely turned off, but I still slept with him several times after that and was considered by many to be his "little" girlfriend, as he had a wife and many others.  I really cared for Mr. Older Man.

I see him every now and then in passing.  I believe he's gotten a divorce in the recent years. Oh well.

# GRADUATION DAY P.S. 31

What in the world was I going to do with myself now?  I mean, who in their right mind was going to hire me? I had a high school diploma and no job experience.

I kept asking myself over and over what good was a diploma, with no skills and kept coming up with the same answer...NOTHING!  It was time for a plan, but not today.

"Kalico, Kalico!" My mother screamed.
I usually ignore her yells, until she calls me by my middle name, which happens on the third... "Kalico Renee, don't you hear me calling you?"
I jumped up out of bed answering, "Here I come." I made my way to the kitchen where my mother was sitting in the window.
"Sit down Kalico, I want to talk to you."

I sat down.

"Kalico, now that you have this diploma, what are you going to do?"
"I don't know."
"Well what do you WANT to do?"
"I want to hang out!" – I couldn't believe I said that.
"What did you just say?"
I repeated myself, "I want to hang out. You never let me go out to any parties or anything. And Charlie, (my younger brother), spends the night out. He goes to the village.  He does whatever he wants and I..."

WHAM! She slapped me, just like that.  WHAM, slapped me.

"Don't compare yourself to him, he's a boy!"
"But he's younger than me." I continued, "Cee Cee and them get to hang out all the time."  Cee Cee was a close friend of mine whose mom took me in as if I was her own.  I later fucked Cee Cee's boyfriend as she laid in

the hospital giving birth to their son. Fucked up, isn't it?  I know, but her boyfriend used to laugh about it, always joking about what would happen if she ever found out.  It made me sick to know he thought it was funny, when we BOTH knew if she ever found out, it wasn't going to be him who would be getting their ass kicked.

To tell you the truth, and this is all true, I don't know why I even slept with him in the first place.  Yeah, he slipped me money at every opportunity, but he was a fuckin' headache and you know what?  In the long run...I didn't gain shit.

"You don't want to go to college?  If you start now, you can be a doctor, a lawyer, whatever you want to be."
"No, I just want to hang out."

My mother had this look on her face like she felt sick.  Her cheeks were flushed and her skin turned some kind of a reddish brownish purple.  She didn't say a word for a few minutes, except when one of my brothers came in the kitchen to get a snack, and she told him to go back to his room and stay there.
Oh my goodness, what was she going to do to me that she didn't want him to witness?  We all knew mom was crazy, but did my need to wander the world send her over the edge?  What was she thinking?  And above all, could I make it to the door or telephone quick enough to get me some help if I had to?

Just then, she looked up.  She had regained her natural skin color and the look on her face changed.  She had this look on her face as if she'd just found out she didn't have three kids, like she was just trapped in a nightmare all these years and our REAL mother was coming to get us.  Whatever it was, I wasn't about to be fooled by that look of relief, I inched my way towards the kitchen entrance as she spoke.

"Okay, so you want to hang out?  You say I haven't let you explore; you're right.  I guess I have been kind of strict with your comings and goings, so I tell you what, you can hang out for ONE YEAR, then you have to go to school or get out!"  She finished with, "Your curfew is 3:00a.m., don't be a minute late!"

I began to jump up and down with excitement.

# When Gucci Came First

"Thank you Mommy, thank you," I left the kitchen.

Thirty minutes later, my mother called me into the kitchen again.

"Oh Kalico, just because your curfew is 3:00a.m., doesn't mean you can hang out all night and sleep all day. You have to get a job if you want to continue to live in this house and keep that curfew. Do you understand me?"
I put my head down. I knew there was a catch to that shit. Did I understand her? Did I understand her? I wanted to say, "No bitch, I don't understand you or this shit you're talking!" and tell her to take her room and rules and shove them up her ass.
But when my mouth opened, "Yes, I understand" came out.
"Good Kalico, you have one month to find a job"

I didn't respond.

"Did you hear me?"
"Yes."
"Now get out of my face!"

I went back to my room, took off my slippers and she yelled out to me, "Kalico since you don't have a job yet, you can do the dishes."

I thought, how could I have a job…its only been five fuckin' minutes. As I washed the dishes, I continuously asked myself why I even fucked with her like that, talking about wanting to hang out and shit.

Hanging out wasn't all it was cracked up to be. Most of the time, I would be sitting over a friend's house watching television or braiding hair. It was almost three weeks since my newfound freedom and my ass still didn't have a job. I kept putting it off to the next day and then the next day and now my deadline was one week away.

I entered the house and announced, "Ma, I found a job!"
"Good" she said.

Damn right, good. I was making six dollars an hour and that was good pay for a teenager. And of all the places to work, I landed a job at a shoe store!

I worked at Parade of Shoes on Central Avenue.
Until I was fired.

 *The 1st Installment of the Kalico Jones Trilogy*

# When Gucci Came First

Fired two months into my employment. Don't ask what happened, 'cause I can't recall those details in full. What I do  remember is my termination had something to do with lying to my boss about being sick and my mother calling the job the same day.  He (my boss) also mentioned something about missing shoes and sneakers.  I'll admit to calling in sick when I wasn't, but as far as the footwear... NO COMMENT.

My mother didn't even seem mad when I told her I wasn't working anymore. I think she just wanted to see how I was going to conduct myself until I started school.

# A FEW WEEKS AFTER MY SHOE STORE TERMINATION I BEGAN MY CAREER AS A PROFESSIONAL HANGER OUTER

I was the hang out QUEEN.  Riverdale, School Street, Whitney Young, Bruce Avenue, I was all over the place and was coming in the house whenever I felt like it.

"Oh shit C.B., what time is it?"
"Four O'clock."
"I have to call home. My mother is probably waiting up for me. There's a pay phone on the corner, pull over."
Ring...ring...
"Hello."
"Hello, Mommy."
She started yelling, "Bitch do you know what time it is?"
"I fell asleep at Lisa's house, I'm about to take a cab home now."
"No you stay right there, I'm coming to get you!"

I jumped back in the car and told C.B. to take me back to Bruce Avenue. I ran up the steps of Lisa's house and woke her up.

"Lisa, please tell my mother I was here sleeping when she gets here."
"Where were you?"
"I was out with C.B. in his new car and lost track of time."

Lisa agreed to do it, but it wouldn't mean anything because just then the bell rang.  It was my brother Joey telling Lisa to send me downstairs.  I walked down the steps slowly.  I saw Joey.

"Is Ma mad?"
"Hell yeah, you're in trouble.  We came over here looking for you two hours ago and all of Lisa's lights were off."

# When Gucci Came First

As we walked down the hill to where my mother was parked (on the corner of Bruce and Lawrence), I started feeling sick. My mother was in the front passenger's seat. I thought to myself, Damn, this is going to be a mess! See, it would have been different if she was driving, then she wouldn't be able to hit me. But with Bill behind the wheel, my mother had free range to do whatever she wanted.

I started to walk slower. My brother looked at me and told me not to worry. He had a plan. He said that he was going to lift up the seat and push me in the back to avoid our mother from hitting me in clear view of all the niggas that were still outside, one of which was C.B.

Joey kept his word. On three. One, two, three, push...Joey threw me in the backseat of the car (he was nice like that sometimes). He and I always fought, but he hated when our mother hit me, 'cause it was like she didn't know how to stop,   like she couldn't stop herself even if she wanted to. My brother stayed kind of blocking the middle of the car so that my mother couldn't get a good shot at me, but even that didn't stop her from trying.

As we pulled off, I heard someone off the block yell for her to leave me alone. She yelled back, "Mind you're fuckin' business!" Bill drove off slowly. I think he wanted people to see me get my ass kicked, in his own little way.

I was so embarrassed.

When we got in the house, my mother was yelling at me. She kept asking me if I thought she was stupid. Now how in the fuck did she expect me to answer that question? "Yes Mom, I think you're stupid?" She can't be serious! So I just stood there, looking dumb, not saying a word because I KNEW if I DID respond, she would loose her fuckin' mind. Here it is, 5:00a.m. and my mother had to get ready for work, and because she had to wait up for her daughter, she hardly slept. Oh hell no, I was NOT going to respond. Respond to a person suffering from sleep deprivation combined with aggravation? No thanks, I didn't feel like getting fucked up. I just stood there, looking dumb, while "yes"ing her to death.

"Yes ma'am...yes...sorry, it's not that I don't WANT to be responsible...I apologize."

WHAM! She slapped the shit out of me. I felt drops of piss trickle down my leg.

# When Gucci Came First

WHAM! She slapped me again and on the same side of my face, too. I started crying. She yelled for me to "take it like a woman!"

WHAM! "You better not cry!"

WHAM! "Take it like a woman!"

"I'm taking you to the doctor to see if you're still a virgin, you do know they can tell if you've had sex. I know you were with that boy (C.B.), because I didn't see him or his car out there when I came to look for you the first time." It was then requested that I go to my room, where I would be on punishment for the remainder of the summer. I couldn't even sit on the porch.

She told me not to even look out the window.

I wasn't going anywhere.

Damn!

Shit was looking real rough right about now. No social life, what was I going to do?

Several days into my punishment, Joey felt sorry for me. He began to let me go outside for an hour here and there, while our mother was at work. That was just his style too. Mr. Big Brother looking out for his little sister, until one day our mother came home early and saw me. I didn't panic either. I just told her I was on my way to the store for a sandwich 'cause there was nothing in the house to eat. She fell for it too. But after that close call, Joey stopped letting me go out. Instead, he would ask if I could go out with him. She was okay with that, but when we got outside, we went our separate ways and Joey was cool with that as long as I met up with him so he could take me back in the house.

Joey, he can be evil, but he has a heart. Shh, don't tell anybody.

"We're moving back to Mt. Vernon!"

My mother made that announcement just as I was getting accustomed to this whole Yonkers thing. I couldn't believe it. I had made friends and everything!  But I guess moving back to the town I was born wasn't so bad (at least that's what I kept telling myself).

# MT. VERNON, NY 10550

Where I would now "click" with Kelly. Actually Kelly and I knew each other from childhood (we both grew up in the projects). We had a lot in common aside from living on South Seventh Avenue. We both enjoyed hanging out and we both thought we were cute.

Kelly and I…we were hanging out all over the place and we had so much fun together. Girls hated us and until I hooked up with Kelly, I never knew any other female aside from me who thought that having girls hate them for no reason was cute. We thrived off the teeth sucking, the eye rolling, and the stares. And when girls tried to bump into us… THAT was the ultimate ego booster, as we truly felt everyone our age wished they could like us AND Jaimie…'cause they wanted to be like her too, right?

But who was Jaimie now? I began to think of her as just another female I could be better than, IF I wanted to, but I wouldn't dare let her know that, 'cause I loved her right? Like a big sister, right? At least I thought I did, up until the night I had sex with her son's father.

He came to my house to bring me some money because the guy I was dating was in jail. Why? Because they were friends and he was doing him a favor, THAT'S why!

I opened the door and looked him up and down. He was gorgeous! Tall with a smile to die for, and a sparkle in his eye. I took a deep breathe and thought to myself, "Why me Lord!" I was too weak to be in the presence of something so tempting.
"Kalico, just get the money and close the door, don't let him in…don't let him in…don't let him in." Yeah, that's what I was THINKING, but unfortunately my eyes were already canvassing the situation at hand, and before I knew it, I began to undress him in my thoughts, right down to his skin. Skin the color of Africa in all it's glory. Skin so smooth you're scared to touch it. Skin so beautiful draped over shoulders built like the mountains

# When Gucci Came First

my forefathers climbed, generation after generation seeking freedom. Damn, how I wanted to be FREE!

Fuck it…I let him in.

But what name can we give him?  Hmmm, let me think for a second…

I've got it…I've got it… let's call him Mr. GTI (since he owned one back in the day). Okay, so Mr. GTI comes to my house to bring me a few bucks to get me "by" since my man was in jail. And the next thing I knew, we were in my apartment screwing like two dogs in heat, and although I'm not going to "spit" the particulars (go in to detail), I will tell you this…1.  The sex was amazing and 2. I had to purchase a new bed-frame the next day.  Why did I do "it?"  I was trying to secure "financials" until my man came home. Period. End of story.

Me and Mr. GTI swung a few "episodes" over the years, but it was always business in some way, shape or form. A few years back, it was rumored that I may have participated in a threesome with him and his man, Five - Two (not fifty-two, just five two), from the "Thug Workout" video.

NO COMMENT.

Three months, three different niggas, and three abortions later, my boyfriend came home from jail.
And it was back to playing "Miss Goodie Two Shoes" and how could I not when the nigga was hitting me off lovely.  Diamond jewelry, full-length shearlings, TV's, and all kinds of shit!

I was 20 years old drinking Moet and Alize, just 'cause the bottles were pretty.  We were wearing custom-made suede suits from A.J. Lester and living large. There was just one problem…I couldn't keep my fuckin' legs closed, I didn't use condoms and since I didn't want any children, I kept getting abortions. I guess that's three problems, depending on how you view it.

So much money, and too much time on my hands.

So much time in fact, I tried to get high again.

# IN THE BEGINNING NO ONE KNEW I WAS SNIFFING COCAINE AND NO ONE WOULD HAVE KNOWN

If it weren't for Mr. First Attempt seeing me and my cousin in Mt. Vernon's infamous 4th Street park trying to score a forty package from a known coke dealer.

Well Mr. First Attempt had the nerve to go to my boyfriend and tell him to get me 'cause I was "in the park sniffing with Carlito."

When Russ caught up with me and Carlito, I was glassy eyed and stuttering. He didn't yell, he didn't scream, he didn't even threatened to beat my cousin's ass (my cousin was a known coke head).  He just looked at me and said, "go in the house!"  I did.

I would be well over a year before I tried it again.

Russ and I...sometimes I wonder where we would be if we had stayed together.

Sometimes, I wonder where we'd be if I didn't meet Mr. Diamond Bracelet.

# STAY HUMBLE STAY LOW AND BLOW LIKE HOODIE, TRUE PIMP NEVER SPENT NO DOUGH ON BOOTY

Thanksgiving 1989

My cousin and I went to the store to get some additional things to go with our family's traditional Thanksgiving dinner at Grandma's house. I'm sure those "things" included beer and soda.

Whatever...

Anyway, we were walking back to the building complex in which my grandmother resides – Lakeview – and a few guys were standing outside. I noticed a diamond bracelet on the wrist of one of them. I thought to myself, "Damn, these kids must be getting money out here. Look at the bracelet on that nigga, look at the ring," I slowed up my walk. Being pigeon with a nice ass was getting ready to pay off for me. I looked back and noticed Mr. Diamond Bracelet watching me and so I took that as an opportunity to do "the walk" – something handed down to me from my mother.

"Excuse me, can I talk to you?" – It worked (the walk) 'cause it's Mr. Diamond Bracelet and he's asking to speak with me. I stopped and turned around.

Now the conversation that followed is a sore spot between Mr. Diamond Bracelet and me. We often try to get it together just in case we have kids or get married and because of the serious discrepancies between our individual perceptions of the conversation, I am not going to go into it with you. But I will say we BOTH agree the only reason I stopped was because of the sparks coming from his bracelet, and the big ass wad of money he just happened to pull out didn't hurt his chances either. We exchanged numbers and would be phone buddies for about one year, eleven months and four days...to be exact.

# When Gucci Came First

In the meantime, Mr. Diamond Bracelet would send me money for my phone bills, jewelry, clothes, whatever I wanted, 'cause I didn't need shit. Remember I had a boyfriend, his name was Russ, so money was truly not an issue for me.

I told a friend about my new venture, Mr. Diamond Bracelet. And since we are now FORMER FRIENDS, I'm not going to mention her name. Let's see, what name can we give her? Hmmm. I know, let's call her Mrs. Mattress Tester from Hempstead, Long Island. We have to give her a name 'cause she's in book two. Okay so moving right along.

I told my former friend, Mrs. Mattress Tester of Hempstead, Long Island about Mr. Diamond Bracelet and she advised me to "go for it" stating that as long as Russ couldn't find out, fuck it.

I concurred.

Mr. Diamond Bracelet and I stayed on the telephone for hours talking about my day at Monroe College (I was in my first semester) and what I did with all the money he sent me. I was happy to speak with him, he was happy to speak to me. I want to say I fell in love with him over the course of those eleven months and four days, but let's just say...I was happy!

Happy until my birthday and he told me that he couldn't make it home to see me. He was in D.C. on business and so I tried to force myself to understand business had to come first. I mean how else was he going to take care of me? Business before birthdays, and I was crushed. Here I was all a mess over someone I'd seen once. I wanted to touch him. I wanted to hold him. I had so many images of how he looked in my head.

I was so attracted to my thoughts of Mr. Diamond Bracelet that sometimes I would forget the fact that I was already in a relationship with someone.

Someone who truly cared for me.

Mr. Diamond Bracelet called me. He said that his plans had changed and he would be able to make it home for my birthday after all. I was to meet him at his mother's house. "Great," I hung up the phone.

"My baby's coming home, my baby's coming home" I tore through my closet looking for something to wear. I was excited.

I arrived at his mother's apartment, looking cute of course, and sat on the couch and waited, and waited, and waited.

I began to worry.

"What's taking him so long?" I asked his mother.
"Girl, I don't know…that son of mine takes his time doing everything."

I could tell by his mother's mannerism that she was used to her son not showing up when he was supposed to.  I, on the other hand, was not.  I started bugging her about her son and she continued to remain nonchalant about him not showing up.  Four hours later, he called.  He was in jail.

"What in the hell do you mean you're in jail?"  I heard his mother say.  To this day, I don't know how he ended up being arrested, but I can tell you this…I was pissed!

He finally made it home, several days later.

I sat in the living room of his mother's apartment, waiting patiently for Mr. Diamond Bracelet to come through the door, just as I had days before.  The only difference was THIS time I told my real boyfriend that I was going to my grandmother's house for a visit.  I had to lie because he wanted to take me out to dinner and I wanted to see Mr. Diamond Bracelet so bad.  Now if you remember, I met Mr. Diamond Bracelet during a visit to my grandmother's on Thanksgiving, and since they lived in the same housing complex, my excuse was "acceptable," and I was cleared for take off, to Harlem.  Russ even called the Touch of Class car service for me to get there.

So anyhow, like I was saying…I was sitting in this guy's house, of whom I hadn't seen since we met, almost one year ago, waiting for him to come through the door, when the bell rang.
It was him.

I sat up and tried to look poised and pretty.  The door opened and Mr. Diamond Bracelet came in and ran right past me and straight to the bathroom. He was in there for forty minutes.

He came out…

# When Gucci Came First

I'm thinking, "Did he just take a shit?"

He sat on the couch next to me and said, "What's up Renee?" I couldn't even speak. I just looked at him. He was fat, he was ugly, and what was that smell? Did he forget to wipe his ass? I couldn't believe the boy I was speaking to all this time looked like this! He had on dirty clothes and clean sneakers. Now I know he hustled for a living, but so did my real boyfriend, and he always looked and smelled good, so I couldn't understand what kind of statement this nigga was trying to make by looking homeless.
After a few hours of talking with him, I decided to look beyond the physical. After all, I was getting a lot of money from this kid, so what if he wasn't cute.

"Look beyond the physical." Yeah, that approach to our association must have really worked, 'cause the next thing I knew, me and Mr. Diamond Bracelet were in his little brother's room on the bottom bunk bed fucking. Yuck! I can't believe I fucked him! How did I let that go down? How was I going to look my real boyfriend in the face when I got home? I came to my senses, quickly gathered my belongings and called cab.

The ride home seemed longer than before.

Oh well, at least I got a chance to think.

The next day.

Ring...ring...
Ring...ring...

Damn! I bet you that's Mr. Diamond Bracelet. I didn't want to speak to him. I was totally turned off, but since I had gotten into a fight with Russ (a few minutes after I saw a pair of boots I wanted), I knew I had to answer the phone. Shit!

"Hello." (it was Diamond Bracelet)
"Hi Mommy"
"Hey"
"How are you doing today, mommy?"
"Fine, how are you?"
"Good"

 *The 1st Installment of the Kalico Jones Trilogy*

# When Gucci Came First

I was trying to figure out how I could keep the conversation light and still get him to send me money for the boots in the process.  I decided to just come out with it, "Can you send me $250.00?"

He said yes, but not before asking me why I couldn't just come down town and get it since he was in town.  I made up something that included a family member being sick or something and it worked, 'cause an hour later, I was on my way to the nearest Western Union location to pick up my money.

I didn't speak to him again that week.

# CLUB 2000 - HARLEM

Kelly and I were out almost every night since we hooked up.  Up seventh and down Eighth...we were trying to break into the Harlem social scene. We finally got our BIG BREAK via Club 2000.  151st Between Broadway and Amsterdam, every Wednesday, hosted by Unique and the Mecca Audio family.

Kelly's birthday was quickly approaching and she just had to have her birthday party at Club 2000.

Me and Kelly on the phone...

"Kalico, do you know what month it is?"
"Yes, it's February...why?"
"And what is February?"
"I don't know, the second month in the year...Black History month... What?"
"The month before my birthday dummy!"
"Okay, and?"
"And I want a party." She continued..."At Club 2000"
"Kelly, how are we going to do that?  Of all places, Club 2000, why?  Can't you can have it somewhere else?"  I was trying to talk her out of it.
"It's there or nowhere...and we're going down there and speak to that kid, Unique."
"When?"
"Today, so get ready Bitch!"
I sucked my teeth, "Okay."
"I'll call you back" (her other line was ringing, as usual).

Okay, so now I have to get myself together.  I knew I had to look good for this.  I grabbed a pair of jeans (the tightest pants I could find) and squeezed my ass in them.  I then located a cutie-pie pair of high heeled shoes, grabbed the bag and belt to match, threw it together with a tight white baby t (with no bra of course).  I looked in the mirror, mission accomplished!  Now all I have to do is sit here and wait for Kelly to pick me up.

I waited.

And waited.

What in the hell is taking her so long?  I dialed her number.  No this Bitch didn't!  She changed her message on her answering machine to say she was called in to work.  Well when was she going to tell me?

I was going to have to do this shit by myself.

I looked in the mirror again.  Okay Kalico, time to go find this nigga Unique. I called Wakefield Taxi and took my ass down to Mecca Audio.  Now for those of you who don't know about Club 2000, Mecca Audio, Same Gang, etc. You missed out on some of the best times life had to offer.  This was a time when "tricking" was in style and niggas didn't have a problem with taking you on shopping sprees and sending you and your girls away for the week.   It was major.

Okay so...

Unique was the nigga to talk to if you wanted to be a part of the "scene" Club 2000 catered to, and being part of the Mecca Audio family was a must (if you wanted to give a party), ESPECIALLY IF YOU WANTED TO GIVE A PARTY.

I walked into Mecca Audio.  It was set up like a game room.

"Excuse me"

No one acknowledged my presence.

"Excuse me."
This time I caught the attention of one of the guys playing pool, he replied, "Yeah, what's up Shorty?"

I looked around.  Damn was this dump supposed to be headquarters? And am I the only female up in the mutha fu....

# When Gucci Came First

"Yo Shorty, what's up…you looking for someone?"
"Yeah Unique"

Shit got silent.  I mean the entire fuckin' place stopped.  The pool game halted, niggas stopped playing the video games and the guy I was talking to walked away from me, and headed toward a window in the back of the room. There was a man sitting behind it.

A few minutes later, the man from behind the window came out and approached me, "What's your name Shorty?"

I assumed he was talking to me, since that's what the first guy called me.  And come to think of it, what's up with this Shorty shit anyway?  I'm five feet, six inches! I don't think that's short, do you?  I answered him, "Kalico."
"Kalico, you looking for Unique?"
"Yes, I want to give a birthday party for my friend."
"Wait right here, Unique is on his way back."

He slid a chair in my direction, and went back behind the window.  I sat down and waited.  And waited, and waited and three and a half hours went by and I was still waiting.  Where in the hell was he?  Shit…it's cold in here and I have to get back home. Time to implement Plan B. I stood up, grabbed a picture of myself from out of my purse and wrote my number on the back of it.  I handed it to the guy behind the window and started to leave.

As I tried to make my way through the door, a car pulled up and out jumped Unique and a girl.  He went straight to the back of the store to the guy behind the window.  I was asked to come back inside.

"You Kalico?"
"Yes"
He looked me up and down and said,  "Turn around."
"What?"
He repeated himself, "Turn around."
For whatever reason it was for, I turned around.

He shook his head, "Good…good…have a seat."

I sat down.

"So you want to throw a party for your friend?"

                          *The 1st Installment of the Kalico Jones Trilogy*

# When Gucci Came First

"Yes"
"She must be some friend."
"Yeah"
"Y'all lesbians?"
"Nah"
"Y'all ain't freaks?"
"No"
"Dancers?"
"Nah, sorry."

I think he was disappointed, but nevertheless he said yes to the party. He would give it and handle all the expenses, all we had to do was hand out flyers. He gave me his number, then instructed one of the guys playing pool to walk me to the cab station, his street name was P-Dog. When we got to the cab station Pierce, oops, I mean P-Dog, handed the driver $25.00 and told him to get me home safe.

I arrived back in Mt. Vernon safe and sound.

# WILLIE'S LOUNGE - HARLEM

Ring...ring...

And before I could say Hello...

"You dressed?" It was Kelly.
"Why?"
"Skeeter is taking us out for drinks for HIS birthday"
"I'm tired."
"I'll be there in an hour."

Did she NOT just hear me say I was tired? I know she did, I mean...I HEARD me say it.  But you see, Kelly had "selective" hearing.  Translation:  she only heard whatever her ass wanted to hear...anything else and she was like a deaf mute.

I started getting dressed for what would probably be an adventure.

TWO hours later...

Kelly came to pick me up. I got in the car.

"I can't believe Skeeter is taking us out and it's HIS birthday"

She looked at me and in a braggadocio manner shrugged her shoulders and said, "Why not?"

And she was right, she had shit on lock like that with him.

We met Skeeter at Willie's Lounge on the far end of 125th Street in Harlem.

So we're sitting at a table, not too far from the bar enjoying our drinks and

# When Gucci Came First

conversation, when we noticed Skeeter was getting a lot of attention from the other men in the bar. Why? Because me and Kelly were acting like he was seeing BOTH of us.

Threesome? Me, my best friend and her friend? Nah, not in a million years, so don't go there. We were just having some harmless fun. THAT'S IT!

So like I was saying, we were sitting at a table, having drinks, conversing about nothing really, pretending to be a three-way couple when Kelly leans over and grabs my arm.

"Kalico, you see that guy over there looking at you?"
"No"
"Stop being dumb, bitch. He's been looking at you all night. He was looking at your ass when we walked in."
"I don't know why, I can barely walk with all these pants you made me put on."

Kelly forced me to put on a pair of long johns and TWO pairs of spandex under my black jeans, because she felt my pants were too baggy, so my butt looked about three times bigger than what it really was.

"Shut up bitch, he got on a Rolex"
Skeeter left the table and walked over to the guy Kelly insists was "checking me out." 10 minutes later, Skeeter comes back and says, "My man wants to buy y'all a drink."
Kelly looked up and responded, "Your man got a mouth?" I couldn't believe she said that, especially loud like that.
"Yeah I got a mouth Shorty."

Oh shit, he heard her. I hope this bitch ain't just start something. And what the fuck is up with word Shorty and Harlem? Well at least I knew it wasn't just a Kalico thing, 'cause Kelly is really short. I don't even think she's five feet, but she's thick as hell, a potential seven on a one to ten. Minus one for height, and two more for attitude.

Anyway, Mr. I wanna buy y'all a drink with the Rolex on walks over and introduced himself and then he looked at his watch in a way that made it impossible for us NOT to notice it. You know how he did it...don't act like you've never seen the "notice my watch move..."

# When Gucci Came First

**Step one...**
He pulled up his sleeve (damn near to his elbow).

**Step two...**
He jerked his arm to kind of make the watch slide down to his wrist.

**And three...**
He held his arm up to the light like he couldn't see the numbers.

**FLAGRANT FOUL!**
**PENALTY:** One, no TWO drinks.

He went over to the bar and ordered three "Mike Boogie's" – a drink named after him of course.

# MIKE BOOGIE

Mike Boogie was arrogant and it showed. No matter what the topic, he continuously based the conversation around him. He always had a story about how something like that happened to him, or how he had been to the place we were talking about or how he knew the person we were talking about. He just knew everything, everything, everything.

And he did too.

He knew how to set up a wide-eyed girl like me.

Just keep bragging about the shit you have.

And I fell for it.

We exchanged numbers and from that night for about 4 months I spent a lot of time with Mike Boogie and once again, I began to think I was in love. I never knew what Mike did for a living, come to think of it. But whatever his occupation, he was good to me.

**WHY IS IT THAT I ALWAYS THINK I LOVE THE MEN WHO TAKE CARE OF ME? DO YOU THINK IT HAS SOMETHING TO DO WITH MY FATHER NOT BEING AROUND WHEN I WAS GROWING UP?**

I'll get back to you on that shortly.

Now back to Mike Boogie...

Mike and I would meet for dinner and drinks during the week. And on the weekends, we would be held up in his Jersey flat, fucking. And the sex... WOW it was out of this world. Mike had this thing about looking me in the face as he came. The first time I heard him yell out "Kalico", looking me dead in the face as he came, made me cringe.  It was damn near scary.  I can hear him now... "Kalico, Kalico, Oh Kalico..."

Okay.  So we had a few good times, Mike Boogie and me and because I was so wide eyed and dumb, I didn't understand the dynamics of fucking with a man like Mike, and he knew it.  He would convince me of how "good girls" stayed in the house, and that my obeying him would be rewarded through gifts, and it was.  Mike spoiled me, until I had that abortion.

Four months later...

Ring....ring...

"Yeah."
"Hey, you"
"Hey, Baby"
"I have something to tell you, Mike, I'm pregnant"
He started laughing and said, "Good."
"What do you mean, good?"
As I didn't think being pregnant with no job was funny.  Oh and being pregnant by a nigga I only knew for four months didn't compliment my situation either.  Damn, I knew I should have used protection!  I repeated, "What do you mean good?"
"I mean good, now you can stay in the house!"
"What?"

I asked, but I knew what he meant. Mike had a problem with my friendship with Kelly, he felt I did whatever she told me to do and that SHE was showing ME too much of the wrong shit.  Little did HE know, that was just the "role" we played around his ass.

"You heard me, now you can stay in the house!"
"If I stay in, how am I gonna see you?"
"I will come to you, now I have to go...I'm in the middle of a business meeting...get some rest for my baby...I'll call you later."

I called Kelly.

Ring...ring...

Ring... she picked up, "Hey girl"

# When Gucci Came First

"Yo what's up?"
I took a deep breath and told her…"I'm pregnant."
"What bitch? By who? Not Mike Boogie!"
"Yup"
"Did you tell him? What did he say?"
"He said, now I can stay in the house."
"No that mother fucker didn't…fuck that nigga, what are YOU going to do?"
"I don't know"
"What the fuck do you mean, you don't know? Bitch you BETTER know. What's his number? I'm gonna call this mother fucker myself"
"Calm down, I didn't say I was gonna KEEP it."
"Well you sure as hell ain't saying you gonna get rid of it!"

I took another deep breath, as she continued…

"Listen bitch, if I have to come over there and take that mother fucker out …" she stopped herself.  Her other line was ringing.  She told me that she would call me back.  I hung up.

In the meantime, Mike called again.  I told him what Kelly said and that she was really upset over this.  He said she was upset because he was taking her star pupil away.  I laughed, then in a serious tone… I explained to him that since I was living at home and going to school, I wasn't prepared to be a mother, and he explained to me how "things happen for a reason," and that upon my fifth month he would buy me a car, an apartment, and a mink coat. But ONLY after the fifth month, because it would be too late for me to get an abortion. In the meantime, if I needed anything, he would buy it for me just as he'd been doing.

I felt better.  He was still conducting business, so we hung up.  What was I going to do? I took a nap.

Ring…ring…
Ring…ring…
Ring…ring…
Ring…

Half asleep, I picked up the phone.
"Hello"
"Bitch I know you ain't sleep…wake the fuck up, wash your ass, we're going

out…I'll be there in a half hour."

Lets' see…thirty minutes Kelly time, translates to about two hours…I laid back down.

And as soon as my ass got to the part of sleep when you're not sleep, but you're not awake either, my bell rang.

Shit, am I ever going to get some rest, I answered the intercom, "Who is it?"
"It's Kelly, open the door!"

Damn, I buzzed her in and ran to the bathroom to wash my face and brush my teeth.  I lived on the fourth floor and since we didn't have an elevator, I knew Kelly would be a while.

I ran back into my room from the bathroom, grabbed a pair of tight jeans and a turtleneck, and Kelly knocked on the door.

"You went back to sleep, didn't you?"
"Don't come in here fucking with me."
"Are you gonna get dressed?"
"I'm already dressed."
"THAT'S what you're wearing?"
"Yeah."
"With what shoes?"
"I don't know."
She went through my closet, picked out a pair of shoe boots and handed them to me, "put these on!"

I snatched them out of her hand and put them on.  Sometimes I think she forgot that I was OLDER than her.  We left.

On the ride downtown, I told her about the car and mink Mike promised me if I kept his baby.

"And bitch you fell for that?"

I didn't say anything.

"If you keep this baby, don't ask me to be the Godmother, don't ask me to baby-sit and don't ask me about no parties, don't ask me to pick you up, you wanna come out with me...NOTHING... and I won't call you back if you leave a message on my machine!"

I remained silent for the remainder of the ride.

Three days later, I got an abortion.

# KEEP IT GOING...ALL NIGHT Y'ALL...

Club 2000, the night of Kelly's birthday party and we were dressed and ready.  Kelly in red and me in cream.

We entered the club from a side entrance 'cause the line was around the fuckin' corner and the street outside the club was filled with cars.

**Shout out to Joe "Black" and a few others from Mt. Vernon** who were in attendance.  We were so happy to see people from our hometown there... Good!  Now at least we had people to go back and talk about the party FOR US.  And it was a party all right.  There were strippers eating each other out on stage, niggas at the bar popping bottles of champagne, and the entire party was singing the Mecca Audio Anthem...

"Keep it going, keep it going, all night y'all, all right y'all and I like to get my dick sucked, I like to get me dick sucked. So what you want nigga...so what you want nigga..."

Yeah, Unique knew how to throw a fuckin' party.

And my man being there made it perfect too. Me and Mike and Kelly with "Mr. Peter Asian and black" ... I think that was his mixture...anyway I won't say his last name 'cause I don't know the particulars behind he and Kelly's affiliation.  Translation:  I don't know if he openly identified her as his girl. But she didn't give a damn about that anyway.  She was just like that, worry free.  That was one of her best qualities.

"Kelly...isn't that one of the kids from Mobstyle?"
"Bitch don't point...yeah why?  You wanna meet him?"

"Yeah, I love that album...You take seventh and I'll take eighth avenue, the location 1 3 2!"
"Oh no Bitch, don't even think about going over there like some groupie, I

know I taught you better than that and besides, it's my birthday and I don't want to be embarrassed."

She grabbed my hand and led the way, straight through the crowd, straight through all the niggas he was surrounded by, straight to him. She introduced us.

He was soft spoken, well mannered and articulate…nothing like the records… WOW!

Sorry… not interested.

But it was nice meeting him anyway.

Okay so, the party was starting to wind down (almost 5 in the morning), we hugged and high-fived each other as we finished our fourth bottle of champagne. Our party was a success!

Two weeks after the birthday party, we were back in Club 2000 and Mike Boogie was there. It was now HIS birthday and he was on his second or third bottle of champagne.

Mike tried to get my attention, "Yo!"

I didn't turn around.

"Yo!"

I kept talking to Kelly who was telling me to ignore his ass.
He walked over. He was wobbly, loud and complaining. My pants were too tight, I didn't return his calls, why was I drinking…why was I in this nigga's face, why was I in that nigga's face. To make a long story short, Mike was making a scene.

I asked his friend Dferge (RIP) to control him and I think he tried, but too little too late…'cause Mike was now screaming at me in front of everyone….."You killed my baby!"
"Mike, please…we are in a…"
"I should slap you."
"Mike, you've had too much to drink, please let's go outside."
"I should kill you like you did my baby!"

# When Gucci Came First

Now as Mike is making this scene, Todd (a Mecca Audio family member) is motioning me to come take a picture with him.

I'm in a fucked up situation.

Now if I go take the picture, Mike is going to become more excited than what he is and if I continue to stay at the bar, Mike is going to keep yelling at me about the abortion. Faced with a decision, I turned to Kelly who said…"Come on, let's go take the pictures, fuck Mike's dumb ass," and we walked over to the area where Mike and I had been just weeks before taking pictures. I posed with Todd.

I knew Mike was going to get mad, but I was starting to go into "it's all about me" mode. You know that mode, when you know you look good and start ACTING like it. I started shaking my ass and doing my little walk and before I knew it, Mike ran up to me and literally tried to punch me in the face! Thank GOD security got to him before he got to me. But that wasn't good enough for me, 'cause just then, I pulled out a razor and we were ALL thrown out of the club.

The following Wednesday, we returned to Club 2000. Todd and the rest of the Mecca Audio family teased me about what happened with Mike.

I didn't find it funny.

# THE SUMMER TIME STROLL

Up Seventh, Down Eighth, from 125th Street to 155th Street, me and Kelly's SUMMER TIME STROLL, guaranteed to fill your phone book or your train fare back.

The "Summer Time Stroll" – that's what we were doing when I met Bahkim and it was love at first sight.  We exchanged numbers and he picked me up later that night. We went to dinner and then to a hotel.  It was supposed to be just to talk, but we ended up using the room for more than just conversation.  So we're laying in this big ol' bed on a high floor in the Marriott Marquis, Times Square when Bahkim leans over and whispers, "I'm married."

Shit! Are there ANY single men left? Well I guess that's better than him telling me he has some kind of disease. And by the way, in case you're wondering… yes, we did use condoms.

He added, "Is this going to be a problem for you?"
"Nope."

And you know what? IT WASN'T!  Why? 'Cause he couldn't ask me shit about nothing …EVER!

12:00p.m…12:00p.m.

I had a talking alarm clock that wouldn't shut up unless you pressed a button. The clock was located on the other side of my bedroom, which meant that I had to get up to turn it off.  As I pressed the snooze button, I noticed the flashing light on my answering machine…I had messages!

In the midst of checking my messages, I realized I hadn't spoken to Kelly since the day before, so I called her at work. She worked with mentally challenged adults and although she was rude and sometimes heartless, she was good with the clients.  She really cared for them.  She did have a soft side,

# When Gucci Came First

deep, deep underneath what she made the world THINK she was.

She answered the phone on the first ring, "Did you have fun?"
"Yup"
"Did you fuck him?"

I didn't say anything.

"I know you didn't fuck him on the first night."
"Of course not" - **I was lying.**
"Good,  'cause you don't even know him."

My other line was ringing; I put her on hold...she hung up.  She was so impatient when it came to being put on hold.

It was Bahkim.  He wanted to see me.  I told him that I had to run it by Kelly first (just in case she wanted to go out too), so he suggested I bring her along.  We went to Tiptin's.

We picked Kelly up and headed for Connecticut.  During the course of our third bottle of champagne, Bahkim directed a question to Kelly, "Would you be ashamed to tell your friend you had sex with me?"

I couldn't believe he said that.  I jumped out of my chair and covered his mouth with my hand.

Kelly yelled, "Oh no bitch, let him go, don't try to shut him up...go ahead Bahkim, I'm listening."
He continued… "Would you be ashamed to admit you had sex with me?"
"No"
"Then why did your friend over here lie to you about what we did last night?"

I thought I would die!

"So you fucked him, why you lie?"
"That's none of your business."
"Oh bitch, don't try to turn this shit around."
"Let's drop it!"
"Okay, but we will discuss this shit later."

# When Gucci Came First

I poured myself another glass of champagne.

Me and Bahkim stayed together for about a year.

Then he went to jail.

Then I fucked his friend.

Well...someone had to take over the bag, shoe and belt bills.

Bahkim was terrific when it came to that kind of thing. He wanted me to look my best and I figured since his friend understood the structure of our relationship, who better to get with? Sick justification number five.

# I BECAME A VICTIM
# OF THE VERY SONG I SING

Next stop...Chaz and Wilson's, a Sports Bar located in the seventies, around the corner from the China Grill in Manhattan and the scene of what should've been my next caper.  But instead I ended up being the victim.

It was basketball season.  I was chillin' with Kelly having a drink, enjoying the live music, when I noticed a few of the Knicks sitting at a table to my right. Trying not to appear groupie-ish, I turned nonchalantly to my left and guess who I saw sitting less than two feet from our table? Fine ass Wesley Snipes. I thought to myself, "its on now!"

Time for plan A: The walk

That's right, I was pulling out the walk. This was an emergency situation and the walk has never failed me. I got up and strutted my stuff to the bathroom. Not that I had to tinkle or anything, but you see, the bathroom was on the far side of the lounge and the "Players Table" was enroute, so I figured this would be a great opportunity for me to test the walk.  Switch hips, bend knees, throw hair back, go...switch hips, bend knees, throw hair back, go ... switch hips, bend knees, throw hair back, go... and NOTHING!

Shit!

I usually get a little something.  What in the hell was happening here?  I looked around and figured out the problem. I was over dressed.  I mean, yeah I was cute, my gear was okay, but the WOMEN in here had on bra tops, cat suits, micro-minis, shit like that.  I was clearly out of my league.  Oh well, at least I know how to come through next time.  I'll just enjoy the music, my drink and relax.

It was 3:15a.m. and I had to go to work in the morning, but Kelly wasn't ready to go.  Damn!

# When Gucci Came First

Luckily the lights came on about thirty minutes later...good... the place was closing.  I had to try to get some sleep so that I could function at work. Under these circumstances, I would have called in sick, but I had gotten a verbal warning for lateness, so that just wasn't an option.  Now calling in dead, that's a thought. Anyhow, I wasn't financially in a position to quit, or get fired, so my plan was to go to work tired.

We headed for the door.

"Stay right here, I'm going to get the car," Kelly said.

I waited outside of the club for Kelly to bring the car around the block.

As I stood outside the club, wanting to be in my bed, I noticed one of my favorite Basketball players. He stood about six foot seven inches, dark complexion and an incredible body!  His shoulders were the true meaning of "hold on" and I wanted to find out.

"Go for it" I told myself.
I walked over to him and said, "I love your game, but why the attitude?"
"Thank you and I don't have an attitude, niggas just don't understand me, they don't want to give me mine, so I have to take it!"

I didn't know what to say.  I just smiled and reached out to shake his hand.

"Well, that's all I wanted to say, it was nice meeting you...keep up the good work."  I turned to go.
He grabbed my arm.  "Where you going?"

HE was talking to ME.  Today just might be my lucky day after all.

"Home."

"Where's that?"
"Mt. Vernon."

He told me where he lived, White Plains – which was only about fifteen minutes from Mt. Vernon.

"Really," I said. "So we're neighbors."
"Yeah, we are...Can I have a kiss?"

# When Gucci Came First

I couldn't believe he asked me that. What am I suppose to say, NO? Yeah right. I looked up and he kissed me. Right there outside of the club, in front of everybody.

"You got soft lips."

I smiled. He kissed me again.

"So, how you getting home?"
"My girlfriend's car is around the corner. She's going to drop me off...I have to work in the morning."
"Tell her to go ahead, I'm taking you home."
"I can't do that."
"Yes, you can."

I walked over to Kelly, who was sitting in the car looking like she wanted to jump out and snatch me up...

"Girl, I'm going to ride with Mr. NBA, he's gonna drop me off."
"Be careful and call me in the morning when you get to work."

I walked away. She yelled out to me...

"Oh Kalico!"
"Yeah"
"I want a 'cut' or I'm telling!"

We laughed and waved goodbye. I walked over the Mr. NBA and WE walked to his car, a Black Mercedes Benz. He put in a tape. It was Heavy D.

"I'm sure you'll like this" (he was trying to be funny).
"I love Heavy D!"
"Hev's my nigga."

He turned the music up as we headed for the highway and then it happened... He started singing. I'm sitting in his car, trying not to laugh, but it was hard. I mean did Mr. NBA think he was one of the Boyz? (Heavy D and the Boyz).

The ride was about twenty minutes, maybe twenty-five, but it seemed longer. I think it was because he kept asking me question after question. Or it could have seemed longer because I was nervous. His line of questioning was different: Do you have a man? When was the last time you had sex? What school did you graduate from? How old are you? Are you shy? What company do you work for? What's you job description? How much do you weigh? SHIT! He asked me everything except for if I was on my period.

I felt like I was under a hot light in a police station. I hope he doesn't talk this much in bed. That would be a turn off.

He rubbed my leg.

"So, you don't have anything you want to ask me?"
"No, I pretty much know everything I need to know about you."
"You sure about that?"
"Yes"
"Well, what do you know?"

I started off with his college and took him straight to his position with the Knicks – Mr. Sixth Man. And he was impressed.

"Wow, so you're a fan, huh?"
"Yeah, I guess you can say that."
"How do you know so much about basketball?"
"My brother Joey, he can play...I mean he's really good."
"Maybe one day I can play him."

We were still on the Hutch. This ride seems kind of long to me right now. I read the next sign. It said White Plains. Damn, he wasn't even going to ASK me if I WANTED to go with him.

The security guy let us into the complex. Hmmmm nice set up. I mean it was decent. Not at all what I would expect of a Millionaire.

We entered his unit.

**WHY DO ALL NIGGAS WITH MONEY HAVE TO BUY A LEATHER SECTIONAL AND A BIG SCREEN TV?** I knew what the bedroom looked like before I even entered it. Always, black or green lacquer and a mirrored headboard. I walked into the master bedroom. BINGO! Just as I thought. It's a damn shame to be so common.

# When Gucci Came First

The tour of his 3-bedroom suite was over and we went back into the living room.  I sat down on the sofa and watched a bootleg copy of Passenger 57 while he played the arcade size video game, featuring him of course!

I don't know what time it was when I fell asleep.

He picked me up and carried me into his bedroom.

Beep.  Beep.  Beep.  Beep.

Shit!  It was 9a.m. and my ass should be swiping my badge at Smith Barney right about now.  I jumped up, asked for a towel and washcloth and ran to the bathroom.  Mr. NBA called a taxi.
But not before he asked me to take the day off.

And NOT before I asked him to call my job for me.

By the time I got to work, news of who called my boss for me that morning spread like a wild fire throughout the department.

My fifteen minutes of fame by association had me thinking I was the shit!  All day, just walking around like I owned the place.  I described to some of the girls in the department, my night with Mr. NBA.

"Y'all should have been a fly on the wall last night...He picked me up, carried me into his bedroom and the things he did to me...have got to be illegal in most states!"

And as if my description of the acts committed to me weren't enough to satisfy their curiosity, don't you know, someone had the nerve to ask me THE question of all questions...

"Does he have a big dick?"
"The only reason I am going to answer this, is because I feel I owe you ladies something after a night like that...YES!"

My Supervisor came over and asked us to "break it up!"

Even though the conversation was over, my thoughts continued. I wondered when I would see him again, and if I crossed his mind since I left, I beeped him during lunch.  He called back, but the conversation didn't last long,

                    *The 1st Installment of the Kalico Jones Trilogy*

# When Gucci Came First

'cause he was getting ready to go work out.

5p.m....time to punch out, go home, and hit the sack.

Kelly left four messages on my answering machine that night.  I didn't return her calls until the following day.
"What's up girl?"

"Bitch, for all I know, you could have been dead, why didn't you call me?"
"Sorry."
"I hope you got paid."
"Yeah, he gave me money."
"Well I need $150 or I'm telling."
"Oh, you pimpin' me now?"
"Yeah Ho, I thought you knew...look I gotta go, I'm about to be late for work...I'll call you on my break."
"Not YOU trying to get to work on time, or even go!  Did you get a raise or something?"
"Ha ha, very funny, now I gotta go and you better get my 150."

She hung up and I turned on the television.

I never did give her that 150.

# TWO DAYS LATER...
# GO SEE THE DOCTOR

The next day for me was horrible!  I kept going to the bathroom, my lower abdomen was hurting and a clear liquid was pouring out of me down there! "What the fuck did this nigga give me?"  I was talking to a girl I met that night at Chaz and Wilson, she's a model and can currently be seen on the Dark & Lovely hair dye box.

"Girl you better see a doctor."
"I'm in the emergency room right now!"

I was on my cellular phone and clutching my stomach at the same time.  I had something and it made me feel dirty.

"How you gonna raw dog a basketball player?  And HIM of all people, he fucked EVERYBODY!"
"How do you know?"
"He used to fuck with one of my friends."

The triage nurse was calling me.  I told Shelly I would call her back later.  I was led to a small room off the side of the emergency room at Mt. Vernon Hospital where a doctor examined me.

"What is it? What did he give me?"
"I don't know, but it's definitely an STD."
"Oh God!"

I was so embarrassed. Here I was twenty something years old crying in the emergency room in front of all those white people, being "labeled."

Two shots in the ass later and a prescription for an antibiotic, I called Mr. NBA.

"Yo, what's up?"

# When Gucci Came First

"I just came from the Doctor."

He was silent.

I continued, "I have some sort of sexually transmitted disease, they gave me two shots and a prescription for an antibiotic…I think you should get yourself checked out so you don't give this shit to anyone else!"

And in a very soft voice he said, "I'll go to the team doctor tomorrow."

I hung up.

Ring…ring…

And before I could even get the word hello out of my mouth…it was Mr. NBA.

"Did you hang up on me?"
"No, I said bye."
"You mad?"
"At you? No, at me? Yes. I should have known better than to raw dog a basketball player."
"Oh now you trying to diss me? You don't want me to call you anymore?"
"I didn't call you to argue, I said I'm not mad, don't worry about it."
I changed the subject. "So whatcha doing?"
"Laying down, watching TV…what are you doing?"
"I'm on Canal Street trying to buy a belt for my brother."
"What are you buying me…or you can't do that?"
"I can."
"Call me when you get home, I want to see you."
"Okay."
"I miss you!"
"I miss you too!"

We hung up. I was really missing him too. Despite the shots and the pills. I was sending him flowers, buying him gifts, taking emergency vacation days to keep him company during his frequent suspensions from the league. I was in love…AGAIN!

Me and Mr. NBA would be together on and off for a few years, and throughout it all, WE NEVER used a condom. Whenever he wasn't on the road, I was at his house. I was focused on Mr. NBA so much to the point that I almost forgot about my OTHER love.  You know the guy I was in love with prior to me meeting Mr. NBA at Chaz and Wilson that night.

So my other true love and I had an agreement. While he was away in College, we would see other people, but we had to use protection and we couldn't fall in love.  But based on the pregnancy test I took just two days prior to him coming home from school, I broke both rules.  Shit!

# PREGNANT AGAIN

What am I going to do now?  I decided to call my friend Jeff from Brooklyn. I needed some guidance from a member of the True Players Association and with all the game Heavy (Jeff's nickname due to his weight) had...he wasn't just a member, he was the fuckin' President and Founder.  I picked up the phone.

(718) 771- ####

Ring...

"Yeah, who's this?"
"It's Kalico"
"Yeah. what's up Kalico?"
"I'm pregnant!"
"By my man playing ball?"
"Yeah, what should I do?"
"You know you can't keep it."
"Why?"
"The nigga just signed a big contract, he's not gonna fuck with you if you try to keep it, he gonna think you're after his money."
"Well, should I tell him?"
"No, but if you do, and I know you will, you start by telling him you're getting an abortion."
"Okay"
"He'll have more respect for you in the long run, because he'll know you're not after his dough... now get on your job and call me back!"

He hung up.

I heard everything Heavy was saying, but I couldn't help but wonder what that noise was in the background.  You see, Heavy kept a revolving door when it came to females and sometimes (I'm lying, quite frequently) I found myself trying to figure out just what it was about him that made him so appealing, this is not to say that Jeff was ugly, because he wasn't – it's just that I never looked at him like that. You see when I met him, in Club 2000 he actually had to save me from all the men flocking around me. He pretended to be security for me. No lie, it was a mess – men were writing me notes on the back of party flyers and bar tabs. Damn, those cream riding pants and boots! At any rate, Jeff was a ladies man and I secretly wanted to know why.

**My pregnancy conversation with Mr. NBA**

"Hi baby!"
"What's up?"
"I went to the doctor today."
"And?"
"And I'm pregnant."
"Yeah?" He obviously wanted me say I was keeping it. I think he expected that, but I had a surprise for him.
"I'm going to get an abortion next week."
"That's what you want to do?"
"Yes"

He offered to give me whatever money I needed so that I wouldn't have to use my own. I accepted and he brought the money to me the next day. He was going to be away on a road trip for eight days.

Damn! Another abortion. This time I wasn't going to let the doctor put me to sleep. Just give me the laughing gas. How pathetic, I know. And the following week, we were fucking again, and still without protection. I guess I didn't learn my lesson.

# YOU'RE GONNA DO WHAT FOR THIS NIGGA?

He sat up in bed.

"Do you have any fantasies?"

Uh oh, where was THIS question coming from?

"Why?"
"Stop being silly, do you have any fantasies?"

His voice was loud this time.  You could tell we were about to get into a serious discussion.

"No, not really"
"Do you know what a Booyah is?"
"No"
"Well that's my fantasy. To see two girls have sex with each other then with me."

Gulp.  I was quiet while he proceeded.

"But I want my girlfriend to participate."
"Really?"
"Do you love me?"
"Yes"

Oh no this nigga was not about to ask me what I think he was going to ask me.  What the fuck did I get myself in to?

"Are you my girlfriend?"
"I guess."

"You guess, then what are you doing here?"

# When Gucci Came First

He repeated the question and started tickling me... "Are you my girlfriend?"
Laughing I said, "Yes, I'm your girlfriend."
Still tickling me he said, "What? I can't hear you."
"Yes baby, I'm yours!" I put my arms around his neck and gave him a kiss.

We made love.

# DON'T FUCK WITH A BITCH
# FROM THE PROJECTS

I took a taxi home, it was six in the morning and I had to get changed for work. Around 4:00p.m. Kelly called my job, she needed to see me, and she said it was an emergency.  I left work and went straight to her house, but there was no emergency.  Kelly called me over for her mother.

Now I am not going to go word for word about what happened when her mother pulled me off that elevator and locked their 8th floor apartment door behind me, only because THIS is NOT about THEM.  Just know that Kelly and I ended up having a mild fistfight and Jaimie was there, as some sort of witness to what I was being accused of.

It was being "alleged" that I may have been fucking Kelly's father.

NO COMMENT.

No fuck it…I will comment…

I fucked him, twice and both times it was wack. He almost dropped me getting into a hot tub at a hotel in Staten Island, he was flabby and kept talking about how my short hair cut looked nice on me, he said it reminded him of a singer he had a crush on. And despite the "situation" he didn't hide me, he took me out and introduced me to his friends and family. It was fun in the beginning, but after a few months of him parking his car outside my house I began to feel uncomfortable, so I broke it off with him.  But did he care? Hell no, he wanted me and so from the day I broke it off with him until the day I moved, he continued  to park that fuckin' old ass Saab 9-5 in my driveway. Shit!

In the meantime, his wife's obsession with me grew. One day I ran into him minding my own business in Yonkers.  That's when he told me about how his wife and daughter to this day  badger him about whether or not we slept together, so much to the point where I think he may have confessed.

# When Gucci Came First

Regardless, I was disgusting for that, just as he's probably still unfaithful.

Fucking your best friend's father, now that's some Jerry Springer shit for real! And I don't think that's funny, nor am I justifying my behavior, so I am going to leave it like this: That was a very low moment in my life, but unfortunately not the ONLY low moment in my life.

I owe her more than an apology. (shaking my head / exhaling)

A few weeks after the shit about me and Kelly's father hit the fan Kelly and I tried to spend some time together – I even threw her a party at Club Scandals in the Bronx (which was a success by the way!), but the relationship was never the same.

You should've seen the look on all those girls' faces when they walked in the club and saw me and Kelly laughing and dancing together like nothing ever happened. They were pissed! And they should've been, out on 3rd Street in Mt. Vernon, trying to fight me on Kelly's behalf not even two weeks before… yeah I could see why they would be just a little mad.

Oh well, time to move on.

# SLOW DOWN
# YOU'RE MOVING TOO FAST GIRLY!

Mr. NBA called me the next day.

"Are you coming over?"
"I don't know, why?"
"Remember what we were talking about the other night?"
"Yeah"
"No, you don't"
"Yes, I do"
"Then what am I talking about?"
"Fantasies"
"What about fantasies?"
"A Booyah"
"Did you think about it?"
"Yeah"
"And are we gonna do it?"
"I guess"
"It's either yes or no. Unless you don't really love me, cause I THOUGHT you did, and if you don't then, what does that tattoo mean?"

I couldn't believe he took me there.   I always ended my letters or messages to him with "...Unconditional" always three dots before the word, always. I didn't want to tattoo his name on my shoulder, so I tattooed the word unconditional.

I later added the number 69 lying down, flipped backwards.  Most people think it's a "cancer" sign, but all my peeps know what it stands for.

Mr. NBA continues... "Do you know anyone who would do THAT for you?"

I was quiet.

"All those friends you got, I know someone would do it"
"When do you want to do it ?"
"As soon as you can."
"Let me make a few calls, I'll call you back."
"Okay, hurry up...and Kalico...I love you."

Yes ladies and gentlemen, I fell for it.  He said he loved me and I fell for it.  I flipped through my phone book...hmmmm let me see...who can I get to do this for me?  I know... I'll call Allie. I KNOW she can help me.

I picked up the phone.

919 – 33# - #### Yeah, it's a North Carolina number...Allie (short for her REAL name), was all "caked out" and living down south at the time, but her reputation still held weight up my way and THAT'S why I called her.  Translation:  She could make things happen for me long distance that I couldn't orchestrate locally.

Ring...ring...

"Hello" (sounded like this...HAAL- LO - WUH)
"What's up? It's Kalico."
"What's up trick, what do YOU want?"
"Allie, I need a favor...I need someone to come with me to Mr. NBA's house, he wants a threesome."
"Oh bitch, you never did that for me! Let me see what I can do...I'll call you back."

Not even five minutes later...

Ring...ring...

"Hello"
"Yo, take down this number...her name is Michelle...she'll do it."
"For real?"
"Yeah...and you owe me one."

She hung up.

I called Michelle and she agreed to participate, damn Allie's pimp hand was long!

# When Gucci Came First

I called Mr. NBA, then I called a taxi. From Mt. Vernon to Yonkers to White Plains. I was nervous.

As we entered the apartment, there was another man there. Mr. NBA said it was his cousin. He said that his "cousin" was there so that Michelle would have some kind of company when IT was over. I didn't see anything wrong with that.

Well Me and Michelle decided that if we were going to do IT, we were going to do IT drunk, but functional. Enter Bacardi 151, the choice of champions!
We drank, and we drank and we drank and now feeling drunk, we went into the smallest bedroom and laid on the floor. Michelle and I had sex, while he and his so-called cousin watched, and then they joined in.

Mr. NBA, Michelle and me. His cousin and Michelle. Mr. NBA, Michelle and his Cousin and then…Me and his Cousin.

Wait…wait…how did that happen?

I still don't know.

The only thing I could think to blame it on was the liquor, it just had us going. I know they say don't drink and drive is rule number one when it comes to what NOT to do under the influence. But rule number two should be don't drink and fuck! Ha ha ha - I'm laughing now, but check out what happens next.

So we're having sex right, the four of us right, "switching" periodically right, then…my drunkenness wore off, I started feeling a little tired and a lot of sick, I left the room.

Mr. NBA followed.

"What's wrong?"
"Nothing"
"Did you have fun?"

Sarcastically I replied, "Did you? It was YOUR fantasy."
"Yeah, thanks!"

# When Gucci Came First

He gave me a kiss and laid down next to me.  We made love.  It was strange though 'cause he kept asking me questions, questions like: Why was I making so much noise with his cousin?  Who had the bigger dick?  Was his cousin better than he was?  And just as I thought his version of the Sixty-Two Thousand-Dollar Question game was over, he started licking my belly button.  Yes, he was getting ready to do the damn thing!  But even that didn't stop him from continuing his slew of questions...he was a professional like that (ha ha ha), he must have been right?  'Cause even THEN he couldn't keep quiet.  He started asking me if Michelle was better than him at eating pussy?  He wanted to know who was the best?  Did I come?  And if so, how many times?  Shit, why didn't he just give me a sheet of paper and a fuckin' pen.  How else was I supposed to keep track of the shit he was asking?

Still not fully sober and dead ass tired, I turned over and fell asleep for what seemed like maybe a half-hour.

I kicked out my leg...wait a second...no Mr. NBA.  I stretched my arm across the bed...still no Mr. NBA, I turned over, no Mr. NBA and the door to the room was closed.  I got out of the bed, opened the door and heard faint moaning.  I searched the apartment.  Bedroom number two – his cousin sound asleep...I walked down the hall to bedroom number three and there they were, Mr. NBA and Michelle fuckin' like rabbits without a condom.  SHIT!

I went back to the master bedroom, got dressed and called a taxi.

Now fully dressed and pissed off, I walked back to bedroom number three to inform my man and home girl of my departure.  Mr. NBA got up and had the nerve to ask me if I was mad with him.

Fronting, I made up a story about how I had to go to work in the morning.

His dumb ass didn't even realize it was Saturday!

I walked out of the apartment.

Michelle came behind me about ten minutes later, and asked me for his number.

I gave it to her.

# FROM WIFEY POTENTIAL
# TO MRS. BOOTY CALL

Anytime I saw Mr. NBA after that it was strictly for sex. Four in the morning on Sundays and Wednesdays, so every Monday and Thursday my ass went to work tired. His calls in between our visits became less frequent, and "normal" sex was never enough.

Sex went from me and him to me and Michelle...to me, Michelle and him... to Michelle and him...to me, Michelle and his cousin... to Michelle and his cousin... then to me, Michelle, him and his cousin... and now...I'm at his house with him and one other person by myself. Is this what I've become, a sex toy? What about my career? My hobbies? Did this nigga even remember my last name? Probably not!

I called my friend Heavy (Jeff) from Brooklyn. He picked up the phone on the SEVENTH ring.

"Guess what?"
"Kalico, I'm getting some head right now, let me call you back."
"It's important!"
"Okay, Okay...Uhh, Uhhh, Ohhh..."
"Heavy, would you stop and listen to me, please!"
"Uhh, Ohhh, Ohhh, Uhhh..."

Shit! I hung up. It was obvious Heavy was well into the situation at hand and although I didn't want to listen to him "receive," I couldn't help it. I had to figure out what it was about Heavy that made females loose their minds.

I listened for seven minutes.

Then I hung up.

23 minutes after that, my phone rang.

# When Gucci Came First

"Hello"

"Yeah, what's so important?" – It was Heavy calling me back.

"Heavy, remember when I told you about me and Mr. NBA and Michelle?"

"Yeah, Yeah and his so-called cousin, I saw them at the Country Club."

"The Country Club?"

"Yeah, Maria Davis' thing...but what's up?  Let me guess, the nigga dissed you, right?"

"I don't know what's going on.  Last night I went to his house and his friend was there from Chicago and we all..."

"Yeah, he ain't fucking with you no more."

"How you know?"

"Kalico, you cant be a player, if you don't know the game."

"What?"

"Buy my book,  it's all there for you in the manual!"

"Heavy stop playing please!"

"You see Kalico, any chance you had of being Wifey is gone...it left when you agreed to bring in the girl, then slept with his cousin, and if that wasn't enough, you topped it off by sleeping with him and his man.  You have no future with him now. You went from long term potential to groupie status."

"Which means?"

"Short term."

"Okay, so what do I do?"

"Shit, you might as well start asking him for some REAL money.  Get paid for what you're doing, since you're a groupie and all."

I felt cheap, but I knew what my friend was telling me was true.  I knew I played myself and I had to face it...the relationship I THOUGHT we had was OVER!  I had to speak to Mr. NBA, I had to hear it from him.  I just had to hear it from HIM.

I beeped him. He called back screaming about being too busy to talk to me, so I hung up on him.  He called me right back and the argument that followed is too painful to revisit, just know that he was cursing and screaming and yelling and then it happened...

He called me "trashy" – and asked me not to call him again.

Trashy!  Trashy!  I called his ass back and left a message.

"I have NEVER asked you for anything...I have always been there for you no matter what...taking days off work every time your ass gets suspended from the team, and let's not forget all the OTHER things you've gotten yourself into…I'm such a fool.  I wish I could erase the countless taxi rides to your house at four in the morning to give you pussy when you were having problems going to sleep by yourself…after all these years and all we've been through, you choose to end it with me like this?  You're a fuckin' coward and you don't ever have to worry about me calling your black ass again, good bye!"

I slammed the phone down.

He called me back a few hours later. His call began with an apology.

No wonder he apologized, I watched the eleven o'clock news, the nigga got suspended again!

# THE "TRACK"
# 28TH & 10TH AVENUE - NYC

Beep. Beep. Beep.

I looked out the window; it was Manny, a cop from Queens that I met on 28th Street and 10th Avenue.  He was with an actor; you know the one, who played opposite his wife in a Basketball movie, prior to their wedding. Anyway, Manny and Mr. Actor were driving around the "track" when we met.  I still don't know what they were doing out there with all the pimps and prostitutes, but whatever...

What was my ass doing down there?  I was hanging out with Dee and Bee Bee, two girls I met through a friend, they were prostitutes.  They called themselves "renegades" because they didn't have pimps. We have a friendship that transcends the demographics of whoring and I would meet them in the city and they would take me to this guy, Big Lee.  He and his family have been in the music business for years. Big Lee... an all around nice guy. No thug, just a nice guy with money who had a weakness for pussy. And I was one of the many females with whom he shared a "weak" moment.

At any rate my friendship with Dee and Bee Bee was nice. They taught me many things, like how to give a good blow job and take a niggas wallet at the same time and one night after consuming one too many drinks, Dee showed me how to take a nigga's NECKLACE while ...oh fuck it... I wouldn't even know where to start.

I went downstairs.

Manny always looked so happy to see me.
"Hey Honey, I'm starving...let's go to Red Lobster!"
"Hello to you too, Kalico."

"Damn, I'm being rude...let's start all over...Hey Honey, how was your day? Can we get something to eat, I'm starving?"
"Everything has to be your way, okay Kalico, let's go to Red Lobster."

Manny...he always made noises during sex and while he was eating, it made me sick, So about 3,000 dollars later and two fucks, I cut him off.

# When Gucci Came First

I should've given my number to his friend, the actor.

"Am I EVER going to have an orgasm?" I asked myself. I am getting so tired of faking it! All this fucking and I never had the "Big O!"

# THE JOURNEY IS ABOUT TO GET REAL PLEASE FASTEN YOUR SEATBELTS

Pro Basketball season was now over and Mr. NBA was playing in a summer league down on the Jersey Shore.  Since his infamous "trashy" comment, we had only seen each other at parties and we barely spoke. Which made his phone call to me a total surprise.

3:36 a.m.

Ring…ring…ring…

"Hello"
"You were sleep?"
"Who is this?"
"Oh you don't know my voice now, you got that many niggas calling you?"

I sat up.  It was Mr. NBA.

"I wanna see you, I miss you."
"I miss you too." I couldn't believe I said that, what was I thinking?
"Where are you…you're in Jersey, right?"
"Yeah, I'm in Jersey."

I guess demographics played a major role in why I, Kalico, was getting "the call" as opposed to everyone else he knew.

"Get in a cab, I'm at exit 105 off the Garden State Parkway."
"Okay"

I jumped up, got in the shower, put on some clothes and called a taxi.  The ride was going to cost me $110.00.

After being on the parkway for over an hour, I arrived at the Sheraton Hotel, he met me in the lobby with three other niggas, asked me how I was feeling

and gave me a kiss.
We went up to his room.

He immediately turned off the lights and began to undress me. He laid me down on the bed and jumped on top of me. He was pounding himself in me like he hadn't had sex in a long time. He kept moaning about missing my pussy and stuff like that. Five minutes into this thing or whatever you wanna call it (sex), Mr. NBA got up and all of a sudden, I felt something different. He could not have lost weight that fast. I opened my eyes.
Oh shit. There is someone different on top of me. The room seemed as if it had gotten darker and I could barely see my hand in front of my face. I tried to get up. Mr. NBA held my shoulders down and whispered in my ear, "You know I'm not gonna let nothing happen to you, lay down." And before I could respond, he kissed me. He was kissing me while someone else was on top of me. Two niggas. Then a little while went by and I felt someone sucking my breast. Three niggas. Then as if that wasn't enough, someone else was rubbing my face. Four motherfuckers and one of them was in two movies and a Nike commercial. I couldn't believe it. I knew nigga number four. I think he went to college with my brother. After a few minutes into his participation, he recognized me too.

He got up.

His dick wouldn't get hard.

I guess that "Don't you know my brother?" question was a bit much for him to handle.

When the EVENT ended, they went back to their room, which just happened to be adjacent to the room I was staying in.

I took a shower and went to sleep.

In the morning Mr. NBA and his pals went jet skiing, and I...I went back to Montclair.

A few days later when what happened finally sunk in, I cried. That was the last time I saw MR. NBA. I can't tell you how he's doing now.

I          really          don't          care,          FUCK          MAS

# COCAINE IS A HELL OF A DRUG

Well, since I was officially done with Mr. NBA, what was I going to do?  I had no man, and no extra income.  I know…I'll call Mr. Diamond Bracelet and see what he's up to.

In the meantime…

My search for a new best friend was going no where fast.  I would hang out with different girls, but no one was like Kelly.  She understood me, I understood her and now I had to break in a new chick.  That's when I bumped into Denise.  We knew each other from camp, she was a few years older than I was, but she looked like a teenager.  We started hanging out.

Denise had her own apartment, so usually after we went out, I would sleep over and we would just drink and talk about jerking niggas.  It was fun up until the night we were talking about cocaine and next thing I knew, we were on the phone calling someone to bring us a "package."  That was the beginning of a social habit I would struggle with to this day.

Weekend after weekend, I would be high.  Then it was Thursday, Friday and Saturday.  Then Wednesday, Thursday, Friday and Saturday, I started calling in sick or going to work with a stuffy nose and drowsy from lack of sleep.  I stopped shopping.  Clothing had taken a back seat to cocaine and my attitude was horrible when I was coming down off a high.  I was turning into a real mess.

So I stopped.

That lasted two weeks.

I even FAINTED one night during a coke binge.

But that didn't stop me either.

# When Gucci Came First

Sitting in my girlfriend's house getting high, package after package, sniffing and smoking cigarettes, when my heart started to race. I was sweating and nervous. I decided to go home and get in the bed. I put my hands on the table for leverage to stand and fainted. I woke up in an emergency room. My diagnosis, heart palpitations, but I'm sure the doctors knew what REALLY led to my visit.

Being cute didn't help my situation either, 'cause all the dealers I got shit from were attracted to me. I slept with a few of them, but it wasn't to get high, it was because I WAS high. I ALWAYS paid for my own shit, but I am not gonna front, extra shit was almost always given to me. The one time I needed to hear "no," all I heard was "yes," and "here, this is for you." Shit, I guess I gotta help myself.

# USE YOUR CONDOMS
# TAKE SIPS OF THE BREW

I didn't feel well and decided to go to the doctor the next day. During the course of my visit with the physician, it was suggested that I take an AIDS test. I did.

A lab technician came upstairs into Mr. Lavelle's office to draw my blood.

My results would be back in two weeks.

If you ever want to know just how long two weeks is…take an AIDS test! Those were the longest two weeks of my life. On the day of my appointment, I called the Health Center and told the counselor that I was not coming in for my results because I was scared. He insisted I come in, he was getting off work at five, but willing to wait for me until 6pm.

Ring…ring…ring…

No answer!  Shit, where is my brother Joey?  I really need him right now.

Ring…

"Hello"
"Joey, I gotta tell you something."
"What?"
"I took an AIDS test and I'm on my way for the results, I'm scared."
"Where are you going?"
"The Health Center."
"You're okay, calm down."
"Well I'm going now."

I left my apartment.

I walked into the counselor's office, my brother Joey was already there, waiting for me.  The counselor located my chart.

"Excuse me sir, can you please wait outside."
"That's my sister."
"Kalico, do you want him to stay?"
"Yes, whatever you have to say to me, you can say in front of my brother."

He looked at my chart.

"Miss Jones, you do not have HIV or AIDS, please use protection EVERYTIME you have sex."

I was happy.  My brother put his arm around me and we left.

That night I couldn't sleep.  I tossed and turned all night, fidgeting and crying.  I was happy, but sad too.

Two days later, I returned to the Health Center.

I explained to my doctor that I had been up for forty-eight hours crying.

He sent me downstairs to see another doctor.  I was given five boxes of Paxil. I think it's for anxiety.  I began to feel better a week later.

AIDS / HIV is a very scary thing, because no one can be 100% sure they are not infected unless they are not having sex.  And unfortunately, people will sleep with someone knowing they have AIDS or HIV. So be careful and save yourself! If someone tries to have unprotected sex with you, they may be trying to pass you something. Why else would they take that kind of risk in this time of crisis? THINK ABOUT IT AND MAKE THE CHOICE TO LIVE.

# SUMMER TIME STROLL – THE REMIX

Up Seventh Avenue, down Eighth, from 125th street to 155th,  the Summer Time Stroll guaranteed to fill your phone book, or your train fare back!  And I had enough numbers to keep me busy for months.  That's how I met Marc. He was getting a hair cut.  Marc and I hit it off immediately.  He was married to a woman from the Islands and from what I was told by him, it was a marriage of MUTUAL comfort.  From that I deduced, he was either paid to marry her so she could get her citizenship or she got pregnant and he HAD to marry her, at any rate, Marc and I got along famously.  I was out on his arm all the time, dinner parties, shopping, the theatre… he was very good to me and I was getting used to having him around and he would have probably been around a lot longer if we didn't have sex.

The Royal Hotel in New Jersey, that's where we were when Marc cried during sex.  He really cried.  He needed tissue and everything. I tried to comfort him, but it didn't work.  When I asked him what was wrong, he kept saying he didn't "deserve to feel this good" and when I asked him what THAT meant, he said he couldn't explain.

Afterwards, Marc dropped me back in the city so I could meet up with some friends for light drinks.  Before I got out of his BMW, he handed me something.  It was his name chain.  I looked at him and said, "It's over, isn't it?"  He said, "I am not going to see you until she is out of my life (talking about his wife), because there is no way I can sleep with you and then go home to her and be the same."

"I understand."
"But please let me be the first person you call if you ever need anything."
"Bye Marc"

My girlfriends were waiting for me and I didn't want to have an emotional "thing" with Marc.  He watched me walk away.

# When Gucci Came First

I never heard from him again.

And I never tried to contact him.

I threw the name chain in the trash after I finished my second bottle of champagne.

Sometimes during the course of my comings and goings, I wonder how he's doing.  I'm sure he's still working his highway construction job, just as I'm sure he's still married.

# A PARTY AINT A PARTY
# 'TIL ITS RAN ALL THROUGH

Coming down Third Street, I noticed one of the bars I hung out at was still open.  I asked the cab driver to let me out.  I went in and sat down at the bar.

"What's up Baldy?" It was an old friend of mine, Mr. Mutual Friend of Gina S. – He called me his sexy, bald headed bitch.  I would have been offended, but the short haircut I had gotten weeks before did look good on me.

He sat down next to me.

"What's up motherfucker, you bored or something?"
"Ha, ha, where you been…you think you too good for us now Baldy?"  He was talking about him, the bar crowd and Mt. Vernon in general.
"You know I do."

And I was so serious when I said that.

At that time in my life, I was only concerned with who a nigga was, what he had and how it could benefit me and since my town was too small for me to fuck anyone else, I took my show on the road. It wasn't that I honestly thought I was "better" than the next chick, but let's face it, there was no "money" left in Mt. Vernon.

So I'm sitting at the bar of the club, when Mr. Mutual Friend of Gina S. pulled out a package and gave it to me.  I went in the bathroom and took a hit.  Garbage… but sniffable.

Mr. Mutual Friend of Gina S. was a dealer, but I can't for the life of me understand how he made money, 'cause he sniffed just as much as he sold. All day sniffing, fucking and drinking, what a life!

I knew I had to get out the bar quick, because I knew it wouldn't be long before Mr. Mutual Friend of Gina S. would start begging me for some pussy. I called the barmaid over to settle my tab.

"So what you doing after this?"

Damn!  Too late, I knew it.  I should have gotten the fuck up sooner.  I shouldn't even be in here.  Why in the fuck did I tell the cabby to stop?  Why? Why? Why?

"Hey Baldy, you hear me, what you doing after this?"
"Going home, to bed."
"Now you know your ass ain't going to sleep."
"Yes, I am."
"How you gonna sleep high…I can look at you and tell you're fucked up."
"Goodbye"

I got up and walked to the payphone.  I had to call a taxi if I wanted to get home.  My ass lived all the way on the other side of town.

There were no taxis available.

Mr. Mutual Friend of Gina S. came behind me, "Wanna ride?"
"No"
"Ain't nobody trying to touch your bald headed ass… now do you want a ride home or what?"

Reluctant, I allowed him to take me home.  When we pulled up to my house, he asked if he could use the bathroom.  I let him in.  He came out of the bathroom and asked me if I wanted another hit before he left.  He didn't even wait for a response.  He handed me another package and of course, I took it and stood in front of the mirror.

"Do you always look at yourself while you're getting high?"
"Yeah, because I don't like a dirty nose."
He laughed, "or maybe you just bald headed and don't know where your nose is."
"Ha ha ha, very funny."

I finished the package and now stand in need of a cigarette and a beer, I looked over at Mr. Mutual Friend of Gina S., he was staring at me.

# When Gucci Came First

"I don't know why I'm nice to you Kalico."

Damn! He was taking me there. Why does this motherfucker always start this – "I care for you Kalico" shit when I'm high?

I replied, "Neither do I."
"Oh you don't feel like talking 'cause you're high, huh?"
"Okay, time for you to get the fuck out!"

He stood up and reached for his jacket.

"Well are you going to walk me to the door Baldy?"

I stood up and led the way to the door. He turned around and asked me for a kiss goodnight. Right about now, I would kiss this nigga's feet if it would get him out of my house. I kissed him. It was intense. Next thing I knew, his hands were in my pants.

"I see you still don't wear panties."

He started fingering me. It felt good. I wanted to feel more. I grabbed his penis. It was hard. He wanted me. He pulled down my pants, I unzipped his. He kneeled down and started to lick around my vagina. Oh God, it felt so good. We were on the floor by my door, my pants were off and so were his. He inserted himself in me. We rolled, we crawled, we were all over the fucking apartment. It was great!

It would have been better if we used a condom.

Shit!

My high started to come down and I was going into "what did I just do" mode and he was going to sleep. Not here, pal. I woke him up, gave him a washcloth and after he finished in the bathroom, I asked him to leave.

I went to sleep three hours later. It was 9:45a.m.

The next few months that followed would be based on drinking and getting high. I lost my job and told everyone that I quit. It was a sweet set up too, with an international magazine. A very respected publication. The termination was solely due to me making too many mistakes and taking too much time off.  In simpler terms, I lost my job because I was on drugs. I thought cocaine was more important than job security and professional growth.  I was loosing weight, eating every other day.  If I had thirty dollars, I would spend twenty of it on a package and four on beer.  I started hanging out with big time drug addicts.  I was disappointed in myself, but I couldn't figure out how to stop this train ride I had started.

I called ACI (drug rehab) and made an appointment, but never went.  I got into the mindset that only I could get myself off this shit.  I had to just say no, but it was harder than it sounded.  I knew GOD wasn't going to help me do anything (find a job or good man), nothing.  And why should He?  So I could make a mess of the blessing?  I had to get myself together quick.  I went back to New Jersey.  I stopped doing cocaine for almost four months.

I was doing well until I visited Mt. Vernon, and within three hours of my visit, I was high again. Four months of being "clean," down the fuckin' toilet.

This was a damn shame, especially since I was getting ready to start a new job.  I began to question why God had helped me in the first place.  I didn't feel as though I deserved it.

Four months of being clean and a new job and I risked it all to get high. Here I was interviewing almost every day for two months before I found this job, shit! What if my new employer asks me to take a drug test?  Maybe this was GOD'S way of showing me what I could have again, if I stayed clean. Maybe the job was something I could use as encouragement to pick myself up once and for all.

A few weeks later, I realized it wasn't.  I was now sniffing cocaine on a regular basis.

There's got to be something I'm not addressing here.  What was it?  I made a list of all the pros and cons about myself, it looked something like this:

# When Gucci Came First

| Pros | Cons |
| --- | --- |
| Smart | Procrastinator |
| Attractive | Low Self Esteem |
| Educated | Nasty Attitude |
| Creative | Hates Criticism |
| Motivated | Lies to Self |
| Giver | Giver |

What was going on with me?  Why was my self-esteem so low?  I was told I had a narcissistic personality.  Do you have any idea what that means?  It basically means that I need to be noticed in order to compensate for lack of self worth and so my behavior tends to be extreme.  Fairly accurate, I guess… right?

 *The 1st Installment of the Kalico Jones Trilogy*

# I KISSED A GIRL AND I LIKED IT

I got dressed and went to a bar and lounge on Manhattan Avenue and I think 124th Street in Harlem.  I'm drinking champagne at the bar with my long hair (a weave), courtesy of the "track master" himself, Dante, formerly of Jewel's on 125th Street next door to the Apollo, now you can find him at The Kuttin' Room, still in Harlem, just uptown. For those of you who don't know Dante, let me tell you, that boy can weave anything! Long, short, curly, straight, shit…he'll weave your fuckin' eyebrows if that's what you want. And Dante had my hair looking like it was coming out of my scalp and I just knew I was cute.  My long hair, black satin mini skirt with matching jacket and a Moschino belt and bag.  Oh the shoes…Gucci.

"Excuse me, I like your outfit."
"Thanks, it's my birthday!"
"Well happy birthday!"  She gave me a hug.  Her name was Lisa, she was a Bounty Hunter.  I left the bar to go sit with her at a table downstairs.
"Do you get high?"
Without hesitation I answered, "yes."
"Well this place is about to close, whatcha doing after?"

I was now faced with a decision.  I knew that if I left with Lisa I would be getting high.  But it WAS my birthday and I WAS celebrating, so it WAS okay, right? I left with Lisa.

While trying to get the passenger side door open to Lisa's car, this guy walked over to me. I looked him up and down. He fit the profile, dark skin with a nice body and not so good looking. We exchanged numbers and I got in the car with Lisa.

"So Lisa, where we going?"
"To the Black Door."

The Black Door, where niggas were dancing and doing drugs right out in the

# When Gucci Came First

open!  No this bitch didn't take me to an after hours spot.  What if the police run up in here?  My ass is going to jail. And isn't she a BOUNTY HUNTER?  Her ass shouldn't even be associated with a place like this.  Maybe she was fronting like all the other motherfuckers I met and her ass wasn't really a bounty hunter. Whatever the case, I wasn't catching a CASE.  Time to fuckin' go, with or without this bitch, I walked over to Lisa.

"Girl, I'm leaving. I can't stay in a place like this.  I can't afford to get arrested, I would never be able to get a job."
"Okay, just let me finish my drink."
"I thought we were coming in here for a package, why are you drinking?"
"I had to buy a drink in order to get a package."
"Well hurry up, I'm going to wait outside!"

She put down the drink and followed me out.

The car she was driving belonged to her husband and since he was in the hospital, we went back to her place.

138th and Riverside, by the park.

I immediately took my shoes off and made myself comfortable like Lisa and I had been friends for years.  I opened the package.

After three and a half hours of drinking, getting high and smoking cigarettes… Lisa said, "You might as well spend the night."

I agreed. She gave me a long white gown with a matching sheer robe.  I put in on and looked in the mirror, damn, I looked like I was on a honeymoon.

Was this her nightgown from her wedding? It sure looked as though it could've been.  I laid down and she laid down next to me. She put her hand on my breasts, I turned towards her.  She leaned over, looked in my eyes and said, "I hope you don't mind, have you ever slept with a woman?"
"Yeah, why?"

She kissed me and began to squeeze my breasts. I was excited, but relaxed. Did this mean I was gay?  Is this why I never had an orgasm?  Did I really like women?  If not, why was I turned on like this?  I laid back and let myself enjoy what she was doing to me.  Then it was my turn.



*The 1st Installment of the Kalico Jones Trilogy*

# When Gucci Came First

I was shocked.  She was moaning and screaming and scratching my back. Was I good at this? Was I now an official a freak?

The morning came and it was time to leave. Lisa and I exchanged numbers and I went on my merry little way.

I only saw Lisa one time after that encounter, but it was strictly conversation and that lasted about ten minutes.  I never visited or called her again.

I don't know how she's doing.

# MR. KING

10/13/96 my tattoo dedicated to Mr. King.  Producer / Songwriter, I met outside of Perk's that night while getting in Lisa's car. Mr. King wrote songs for many famous singers…and even won a Grammy…I won't go any further than that!

Our first date.  Mr. King picked me up in Mt. Vernon, he was driving a Lexus.

I gave him a hug.  We went back to his house in Jersey.  Being in his presence that night changed my life.  He read to me.  He recited passages to me.  He played the piano, he even suggested certain books for me to read.  We sat up all night watching a tape of a religious scholar giving a lecture.  It was interesting.

I would spend weeks at a time in Jersey with Mr. King, traveling to and from work, I practically lived there.  Everything was nice in my life!

Everything was finally going well, until we I asked him for money.  After that, we starting seeing less of each other.  He was tired, he had a meeting, he was working with this one and that one or he had to go to Los Angeles.  There was always a reason why I couldn't see him.  After two months, I stopped calling.

It would be over a year before I saw him again and without any regard for where we were or who he was with, I asked, "Do you still have my Versace Jeans and gold bracelet?"
"Yeah, 'cause I knew that one day I would run into you and you would come at me with that."

"What's that suppose to mean?"

"It means that's why I stopped fucking with you.  You always wanted to spend money, take me here, buy me this and I've been holding on to those goddamn jeans for this very moment…they're in my car, I'll be right back!"

He got up and left. Low and behold, five minutes later, I have the size 28 Versace Jeans in my hand and the gold charm bracelet purchased for me by Russ. Damn, I must have been some bitch to deal with. Why else would this nigga be riding around with my shit in his car, and well preserved might I add.

Now on a normal, Kalico moment, I would've went there, but I didn't want to make a scene where we were because of all the undercover patrons. It was the least I could do, I mean after all, we were in Harlem Heat (a strip club).

That's one thing about me and just the way I am in general. I can go ANYWHERE. To my boyfriend, I'm his homeboy, his lover, and his babysitter. it's' crazy and we love each other, but we both agree…it's difficult being in a relationship after the novelty wears off.

# IT'S A BIRD...IT'S A PLANE...
# IT'S MR. ORGASM

Oh my God, what's happening to me?  My legs were shaking; I was beginning to feel crazy.  My back lifted up off the bed, and I was pulling my hair out.  I felt like that lady in the movie Ghostbusters, you know the one who floated up off the bed, I think she was the Gatekeeper.  I felt something coming.  Something was happening.  I was about to experience the "Big O."  Oh Shit!  Oh Shit!  I screamed so loud, I KNOW his neighbors heard me.

I jumped up when it was over.

I picked up the phone and dialed my friend Heavy from Brooklyn.

(718) 771 ----

Ring...ring...ring...

"Hello"
"Heavy it's me, Kalico"
"What's up?"
"I did it, I did it!"
"Did what?"
"Jumped the fence!"
"How do you feel?"
"Great!"

I sounded like Tony the Tiger, you know from the frosted flakes commercial.  Ha ha ha...wow!  I felt like calling all the niggas I slept with and cursing them out!  Was this what I'd been missing all these years?  Damn!  You mean to tell me that not one nigga cared enough about me to make sure I was being sexually satisfied?

I started thinking...

# When Gucci Came First

Maybe it was me, cheating myself out of a wonderful experience, by faking all the fucking time. Trading in what could've been wonderful experiences for the obtainment of material possessions? And so that makes me just as selfish as the men I'd been sleeping with. Was my body not worth more than a Gucci bag and belt? I can't believe I had taken a back seat to material shit. Whatever happened to Kalico Jones, the nice girl from Grimes Center for Creative Education? You remember the one who held her own in Ballet, Tap, Photography and Chorus? When did I throw all the things that were instilled in me as a child, out the window? And could I ever go back? Was there such a thing as starting over? Is it possible to re-"virginize" yourself after doing so much? Was I able to get off drugs without help? And wasn't it solely up to me, and what I felt in my heart? I believed I wanted to do all these things. I knew I could. So why couldn't I?

Maybe my new boyfriend would be a good thing for me. He is a health food nut, a straight vegetarian. Only organic food, vitamins and herbs.

He works out everyday and participates in a basketball league at the Y on 14th Street.

I can't say we're going to be together by the time this book is published, but I will say this, he will never be forgotten. Eighteen orgasms in two weeks. I'm surprised I didn't end up in the hospital.

Can someone please tell me why I couldn't feel my legs at one point? If you know the answer to that, write me!

After my orgasmic experience, I made a decision to get my life in order, to get to the root of my issue. I wanted to figure out why my life was in the whirlwind that is was, and I didn't want sympathy or pity, I just wanted to know for myself that my life was "save-able."

# DON'T TOUCH ME THERE IT HURTS

But what was I not dealing with? What was I not focusing on? I knew there was some kind of underlying problem I needed to address.  I closed my eyes and tried to focus on the first image that popped into my head.  It was me and three boys my mother had paid to baby-sit us.  They were brothers.  I recall how one of the brothers would put a sheet over his head like he was a ghost and chase me around our ninth floor project apartment.  I was ten years old and ran pretty fast to be pigeon-toed. You should've seen me running from "Boo" dipping between my brother's bunk beds and hiding in my mother's closet, he never could find me.

Until…

Until, that one day my mother locked her bedroom door before she left out and I had to hide in my brother's room.  I remember that day as if it were yesterday.  That was the day "Boo" caught me during our game of hide and seek.  That was the day my life changed, the day the sexual abuse began.

Everyday while my mother was at work, another game of hide & seek. I told him that I didn't want to play anymore, that I didn't like to play hide and seek with him, but he didn't listen. He would come in, put a sheet over his head and I would try to run and hide, praying that this would be the time he couldn't find me.

But, it was like I couldn't even hide anymore, because each time I would run from him, he wouldn't even count to ten, he wouldn't even give me a chance to run and hide, he would be right on my heels, grabbing me around my little waist and pulling me close to him and kneeling down to become head to head with me in height. What is he doing to me? I pushed him away as he tried to put his tongue in my mouth.

"Get off of me…where are my brothers?" He just laughed about sending my brothers outside to play as he felt my chest and kissed me. I was only

# When Gucci Came First

ten years old, I wasn't even developed yet.  What could he possibly find sexually attractive about a ten-year-old?  What?  And if that wasn't enough, he incorporated his brother into the sickness.

Three very sick brothers who thought they were just fucking with one of the neighbor's children, THREE BROTHER WHO DIDN'T UNDERSTAND the damage they were actually doing to me and how their disgusting acts would affect my life. And I wasn't the only one, after speaking with others in the building – we're all adults now, I am aware of one other girl they abused and she told me there could possibly be a third.

They were so cavalier with their abuse, their friends, our next-door neighbor, everyone knew what these brothers were doing to me and no one ever did a thing.

One time while I was in my mother's room watching television sitting on her bed, the older brother came in and sat on the radiator, the younger brother went next door to get the boy who lived there. When the boy from next door entered my mother's room the older brother said, "Hey, watch this," he pulled down his zipper and grabbed my hand. He asked his brother to close the door.  My neighbor looked on in what I thought was repulsion, but he didn't stop them either.

After the younger brother closed the door, he began to rub himself against me and put his fingers up my skirt. The older brother, who was still sitting on the radiator with his penis out through his zipper guided my hand up and down his private, then he told the neighbor to look as he grabbed the back of my head and told me to open my mouth.  I was fuckin' ten years old!  My neighbor ran out of the room, out of the apartment and down the steps.  He was clearly upset, but he NEVER said
a fuckin word.  He never tried to help me and until we moved out of the projects, I would be sucked on, fingered, kissed and forced to have oral sex by three brothers.

There was an incident, just before we moved…My mother came home earlier than usual and found me  between the legs of the younger brother.

She walked into the room and said to my sitter, "Okay ---- thank you, you can leave now." He let himself out. As I heard the door close, I glanced over at my mother who had a belt in her hand. My heart started to race, what did I do? Why is she mad? She grabbed me by the arm so I couldn't run and began to strike me with the belt. Each time I let out a scream, she yelled, "Did he touch you?" I begged her to stop, but she wouldn't, she struck me with the belt again, "Did he touch you?" "Please mommy, stop..." I looked down and watched the bruises surface on my legs. She hit me again, "Did he touch you?" And in my loudest cry I yelled, "NO!" - She put the belt down.

How could I say yes? How could I tell her anything? How could I? I began to hate my mother. The hate that manifested from that beating developed into a totally dysfunctional relationship between my mother to this day. Sometimes I would look at her and feel sick. I just wanted to ask her what in the hell was she going through that made her forget she was raising a little girl?

On my 26th Birthday, I asked my mother why she never did anything to stop what the downstairs neighbor's sons were doing to me. Her response, "I asked you and you said no!" I went to my brothers and told them because I really thought I was in the beginning stages of a mental breakdown. I won't go into my brother's responses, but just know they feel my pain.

As for my dear "baby sitters," the brothers, one died a violent death, thrown from the roof of one of the project buildings we lived in, the other two are in jail – one for rape, the other for drugs and the on looker, who did nothing, died a violent death also. He was shot in the chest up the block from where we grew up.

May God have mercy on their souls.

# DO YOU KNOW WHERE YOU'RE GOING TO DO YOU LIKE THE THINGS THAT LIFE IS SHOWING YOU...WHERE ARE YOU GOING TO...DO YOU KNOW?

Maybe being sexually abused my babysitters, combined with being beaten by my mother to the point of whelps and bruises and abandoned emotionally by my father, I never really had a chance.  Suicidal thoughts began to occur daily since I began to face my problems.  I was crying all the time, and moody.

Facing abuse you suffered as a child, in your adult years takes a toll on you mentally. I not only had to face what happened to me, but I had to understand how those experiences affected my life.  The abuse definitely had a lot to do with why I went from man to man, totally emotionless, without any regard for my safety or health.  There was a definite correlation between my actions, attitude and what I had been through.  How else, or rather, why else, would I being the smart girl I am allow myself to indulge in such reckless behavior, right?

Absolutely.

I learned that the drugs and alcohol were my way of punishing myself.  I didn't love myself.  Oh yeah, I knew everyone, I had nice things and I looked good, but everything was EXTERNAL and because of that, everyone I knew thought my life was great.   And so how was I supposed to tell people who admired me that I want to kill myself?  How do I explain that I am sick?  Just do it, right?  That's what I did and guess what...

"What do you mean you want to kill yourself?" Leah said.

"See, that's why I didn't want to tell you."
She put her arm around me, "I'm sorry Kalico, but you threw me a loop."

What the fuck was that supposed to mean, I threw her a loop?  Here I am on

# When Gucci Came First

the brink of whatever kind of breakdown this is and the one person I decided to confide in couldn't come up a level and listen to me.

With a smirk on her face, Leah said, "Kalico, you have everything, an apartment, a degree, clothes, looks, why are you even thinking like this? Maybe you should lay down."

I went into her daughter's bedroom. I don't know why the fuck I laid down. I didn't have a headache or anything. I guess I laid down to get the fuck out of her presence. I heard her make a phone call.

"Yeah girl…she's in the room laying down."

I sat up, she was talking about me. I tuned it.

"I don't know, maybe the bitch is high…you know she sniffs coke."

Oh God, who was she telling my business to? How could she take things I told her in confidence outside of our friendship? I heard her laughing.

"She just better not kill herself in my house. She can take that shit home, I only got one daughter!"

I heard just about all I wanted to hear at this point. I made some noise so she would get off the phone, it worked.

"See you later girl, I gotta go…Kalico's here and she doesn't feel well."
I walked into the kitchen. She hung up. How could I stay at this bitch's house after what she just did without slapping her? I planned to stay for the weekend and I did, but I never brought up how I was feeling again. I also had proven to myself that I had grown as far as my temper was concerned, 'cause up until two years ago, I'd stop a party for less shit, so to me not slapping her ass, was a sign of maturity on my part.

Sunday afternoon, she drove me home. I didn't say one word during the drive. I knew I couldn't tell her a damn thing else. She kept asking me if I was okay. I said yes.

I never confided in her again. And our friendship was never the same.
It never will be.

# When Gucci Came First

I think she's noticed that.

I must admit, for about three days following, I couldn't help but to wonder just how much of my personal business that bitch divulged to other people. I knew she had to say other things about me, because she spoke so coldly of me and she was even laughing. Was she just as jealous of me as everyone else? Was she getting a fuckin' kick out of my misery? Was she enjoying this shit? This is the part where I call her a slum dwelling, ten-dollar ho, but I'm not! I'm above that, right? She'll get hers one day and it will be in a form much deeper than someone telling her fuckin' business.

I changed my beeper number.

I changed my phone number.

I changed my friends.

I've forgiven her since then, but only in the eyes of the divine energy and myself. I have no need to call her and tell her how I feel. I'm sure deep down, she knows there is no friendship between us.

I started sleeping all day. I lost my appetite. I didn't want to go out anymore. I stopped dating. I stopped shopping. I started drinking.

Beer or champagne, one extreme or another. That was just like me. Gucci shoes or Payless. I wasn't going to look like I was trying. It was either I WAS or I WASN'T!

Everyday a beer, every night a bottle of champagne. Then three or four beers and two bottles of champagne. Getting drunk cost just as much as getting high, even more sometimes. I knew I was going through some sort of depression. As much as I hate to admit it, I was depressed. And after my dear friend turned my thoughts of suicide into funny conversation with her friend, I felt like I had no one to turn to. I wanted to tell my family, but how could I without them looking down on me? How could I tell anyone? It was embarrassing. My ego was still bigger than my situation.

I called my doctor's assistant Anne. She wasn't at work, so I left her a voice message. I was drunk when I left the message and can't recall what I said to be honest with you, but I'm glad I made that call drunk, because I know if I was sober, I would NOT have done it.

# When Gucci Came First

Two days later, Anne called me back, "Kalico"

"Yes"
"This is Anne."
"Hi"
"Kalico, what's going on with you?"
"I don't know."
"Kalico, I want you to check yourself into the hospital."

We talked for about fifteen minutes and came up with an alternative.  I would come see her on Friday and we would walk over to psychiatric emergency, if she couldn't find a therapist to see me that day.  When I arrived at Anne's office, she called someone she knew and set up an appointment for me.

 *The 1st Installment of the Kalico Jones Trilogy*

# SESSION NO. 1 WITH THE THERAPIST

"I wish I was a bird."
"Why?"
"I don't know."  I looked up at the ceiling.  I felt a lump in my throat. I
started talking to myself, "Kalico, you better not cry" – what's he gonna
think?  I tried to stop my tears before he noticed.  I don't think it worked.
"I just wish I could fly away."
"From?"
"Everything…every time I see a plane taking off or birds, I get emotional.  I
always think to myself, I wish I was on that plane or I wish I could fly…I'm
gonna live in California one day."
"Is that where you want to be Kalico?"
"Yeah, but with my luck, the plane will crash."
"Why do you say that?"
"I don't know."

But I did know.  California represented a new start, an attempt at happiness
and for some reason, I felt as though I didn't deserve to be happy.

I had sixteen minutes left in my session, but we didn't spend them talking.
I had to fill out paper work.  You know, insurance information and shit like
that, then I left.

I thought about my session the rest of the day.  What did it mean? What was
THAT suppose to do for me?  And wasn't I supposed to be lying on a couch?
And WHO was this doctor anyway? But most of all, I thought about why I
felt the plane would crash on my way to California.  Why did I feel as though
I didn't deserve to be happy?

That would be the focus of my next session.

# SESSION NO. 2 WITH THE THERAPIST

"Good afternoon Kalico."
"Hey"
"How is your week going?"
"Fine.  I would like to pick the topic for today, can I do that?"
"You can do whatever you want.  What do you have in mind?"
"California"
"You mean your trip?"
"My trip.  I have been thinking about it a lot lately.  Specifically trying to figure out why I said the plane would crash before I could get there to start my life over."
"Okay"
"Why would I say that?"
"Why do you THINK you said that, Kalico?"

If I knew, would I be sitting in this office?  If I had the answer to my own questions his ass would be out of a job.  I replied, "Do you think it's because I don't think I deserve to be happy?"
"Do you?"

I was becoming frustrated.  Why isn't this mother fuck…no Kalico, don't go there.  Okay, but why isn't he answering my questions?  Why is he redirecting my questions back to me?  What was that going to accomplish? And did I have a PhD and didn't know it?

"Of course, shouldn't everyone be happy?  I mean…doesn't everyone DESERVE to be happy, no matter what they've done?"
"What have you done?"

Shit! What am I supposed to say now?  Do I say I'm a drug addict?  Do I say I'm a whore?  An alcoholic?  What should I say?

"Kalico, we'll talk about this next time."

# When Gucci Came First

My fifty minutes were up, it was time to go.

And not a moment too soon.  At least this gave me seven days to think about what I was going to say.  Or seven days for him to forget.  Nah that's unlikely, especially since he was taking notes.  Shit!

# STACIA

Why did I feel I didn't deserve to be happy?  I asked myself that question over and over.  Why?  I went to Mt. Vernon.  I ran into Stacia.  She's saved now.  That means she asked God to forgive her sins and now she's trying to live righteous.  Stacia, she's a whole new person now, I envy her.  We were on the same side of the street.

"Hey Stacia!"
"Hi baby, Kalico you know Jesus loves you and I love you too."

I started crying right there on Fourth Avenue and First Street.  I always found myself crying whenever I saw Stacia, Cathy or Harvey.

"You know, I was right where you are Kalico."
"But I've done so much"
"It doesn't matter what you've done Kalico, HE (God) forgives you. You just have to forgive yourself."

She wiped my face, Stacia is just like that. Very loving, very loving.

I was so into what was going on between Stacia, God and me that I forgot we were on Fourth Avenue, the busiest street in Mt. Vernon.  Stacia gave me another hug.

"I love you Kalico, and I know you love yourself!"

She put a piece of paper with her number on it in my hand.  I cried my way back to the projects.

I don't think Stacia understood how much I needed to hear an "I love you." I don't think she understood how much that hug meant to me and she probably will never know. A hug and an "I love you" from someone who I have NEVER done anything for.  A person who had parts of my life and pieces of my situation was telling me and showing me (by example) that I would be okay, and that all I needed was to have a little faith in myself.

Faith – the one thing no one could give me and the only thing money couldn't buy.

I went out that night and got high and by the end of the next month, I was known as an undercover "coke-head" and during an argument with someone who I THOUGHT was a close friend, I was called one to my face!  It wasn't there goes Kalico, her outfit is nice, I wonder how much it cost?  It wasn't there goes Kalico, who's car is she driving…is that a Lexus?  It WAS there goes Kalico, her shoes are fly, but she's on drugs.  It WAS there goes Kalico, she looks nice, but she's getting high now.  It WAS there goes Kalico, who was stupid enough to let her drive his car, he must not know she's a coke head, I hope she doesn't get into an accident.

Shit done changed (Ebonics).  I knew all the stuff I was doing would result in bullshit.  I knew this day would come eventually, but I thought I'd get my life back on track before anything hit the street, right?

Wrong!

# EXTRA...EXTRA...HEAR ALL ABOUT IT!

My business couldn't hit the street fast enough.  Everyone with a phone in my hometown was talking about me, why?  What the fuck was the fascination?  Why did people want to see me hit rock bottom?  I couldn't figure that one out, but being that I kept drinking (excessively, I might add) and doing cocaine, it wouldn't be too long before they got their wish, or would they?

First Mr. Diamond Bracelet went to jail, then Mr. Moore went to jail, so extra money wasn't coming in like it used to.  I was frantic, scared, and on the brink of having to budget.  I didn't know what to do.

Damn...I sat down on my bed and looked up at the ceiling. Why did Mr. Moore have to be in jail? I missed him so much. I missed our seafood and champagne nights. I missed the way my stomach would jump each time he smiled at me.  Me and Mr. Moore...we could talk about anything, we had so much in common. I remember one time, after he was out all night with a famous designer and a top fashion model, he picked me up from my "stash" apartment in Mt. Vernon, and...You know what?

I'm not even going to go there.

Let's just say that even if you subtract the jet skiing and impromptu champagne fights, Mr. Moore was still a lot of fun.

There was only one thing wrong with him.

He fucked with Kelly. But fuck her, she wasn't my friend anymore...now was she?  And besides that...quiet is kept...I met him first. I laid back on my bed and started to cry.

Ring... ring... ring...

Who could this be?  I picked up the phone.

# When Gucci Came First

It was an automated voice…

"You have a pre-paid call from and inmate at a federal prison, press 5 to accept…"

My mood instantly changed, it was Mr. Moore calling.

I pressed five.

"Hello"
"What's up?"
"Nothing"
"What are you doing in the house?  I didn't think I was going to catch you."
"Bored…lonely…broke"
"Kalico, why are you broke?"
"I'm not working, you're in there…hello…where is the money coming from…anyway, how are you doing in there, you okay?"
"I'm alright, trying to hold my head until my trial."
"Where are you?"
"Maryland"
"I should come see you."
"Okay, I'll send you the form, but lets not talk about that…Kalico, get a job!"
"What?"
"Get a job! Now I gotta go, my minutes is low cause I'm calling my attorneys a lot, I'll write you and send the form this week."

He hung up.

Mr. Moore was right, I was going to have to get a job.

So, I dusted off my degree in Business Administration and did just that.

# GOT ME WORKING WORKING DAY AND NIGHT

Working.  It used to be an option, now it was a MUST do.  I hated that. I went to work feeling as though someone had a gun to my head.  Every morning, my alarm clock would go off and there would be this person with a gun to my temple saying, "time to go get my money, bitch!"  I hated working, but with my two guarantees being in jail, I had no choice.  When I got to work, I felt like a hostage.  "Kalico do this, Kalico do that" or "Kalico take a message, Kalico I need that proposal on my desk before lunch" – "Kalico, Kalico, Kalico."  It made me sick to my stomach!  For months, I would get up with a gun to my temple. Day after day, "time to go get my money, bitch!"

Shit!

What was so powerful?  What had me working at a place with a person who spoke to me in a manner so harsh and condescending?  I despised my boss! What did I turn my power over to? What had this kind of power over me?

Drugs.

Damn, was THIS rock bottom?  Me realizing what I was doing to myself.  I thought so, but I was wrong again.

I went to church that Sunday.  I liked the message, but people were so into who was there and what they were wearing, it was pathetic.  Now being the daughter of a Minister, I know you're not suppose to go to church for the people, but I needed personal attention.  I needed to be able to talk to my Pastor, Minister, whatever.  I needed to get involved in programs and activities.  I needed something to keep my ass busy.  But I was told I had to be a church member for two or three months before I could even volunteer my time to the church or participate in activities, but that didn't stop them from sending me envelopes for the one thing I COULD participate in... TITHES.  I had a number too, so they could identify who sent what. I never went back to that church.

# SESSION NO. 3 WITH THE THERAPIST

"Good afternoon Kalico"
"Hey"
"How was your week?"
"Fine and yours?"
"Good, good"

I smiled.   He just looked at me kind of strange.  Yeah motherfucker, I'm gonna analyze your ass now.  I didn't have time to think of how to answer the infamous, "what have you done, Kalico" question.  My instinct was telling me to be inquisitive of his life.  Redirect the questions he redirected to me, back to him.  We were going to get nowhere yes, but maybe he would back up off the Califarnia questions.

He took out what I assumed was my life.  Flipping through the pages, he looked up.

"Last week we were discussing what you've done in your life that may have you thinking you don't deserve to be happy."

I looked at the ceiling.

"Is there something wrong, Kalico?"
"No it's just that I don't want to get into my personal business."

Oh shit.  Did I just forget WHERE I was?  What in the hell was I doing in a psychiatrist's office if I DIDN'T want to get into my personal business?  I started laughing.  I see all those drugs didn't fuck up my sense of humor, or did it?  I don't think the therapist found my response humorous.

"You found that funny?"
"I don't know why I said that.  It's just that I feel, that's very personal, you know."

"No, that's why I asked you."
"Oh"
"Kalico, do you trust me?"
"Yeah"
"As your therapist?"
"Yeah"
"Everything you say to me is confidential, you do know that right?"
"Yes"
"Not EVEN the doctor who recommended you to me will know of our conversations."
"Okay"
"But I can't help you if you don't trust me."
"I trust you, but it's disappointing."
"There isn't anything you CAN'T tell me."

He seemed sincere, but wasn't he SUPPOSE to appear that way? Why was I afraid to tell him? I started breathing hard. Oh no, I was having an Anxiety attack. He got out his seat and verbally instructed me on breathing techniques to calm myself down. I was fine ten minutes later. My fifty minutes were up, it was time to go.

He gave me some literature on coping with those kinds of attacks.

Later that week, I went to Bible study at a small church on Fifth Avenue, led by Pastor White, it was interesting – a big difference from the first church. This was a church with people who didn't have much money or many material possessions, but they had faith and spirit and they were family. I liked that. Since it was a small church, there weren't many organizations, but they were close knit, so that would make up for the activities I felt I so desperately needed. Too bad I didn't continue to go.

I don't know why I never returned to that church. I couldn't figure out why I wouldn't let myself be happy. Why couldn't I allow myself to receive a blessing? I thought about my friend Stacia for a couple of days, but I never called her. I thought about calling Cathy, but I didn't. I was jealous of them, being born again, coming out of this life and succeeding. I felt bad about envying them. What kind of person envies someone for finding Jesus Christ? I should be happy for them, right? And I am, I really am, but I guess I wish I had the will power and faith they had.

# SESSION NO. 4 WITH THE THERAPIST

"Hello Kalico"
"Hey Doc"

I started laughing.

"How was your week?"
"Great and yours?"
"Good, good"
He paused, and continued, "So your week was great?"
"Yup"
"Well tell me, what did you do?"
"Went to a couple of parties."
"I take it you had fun."
"Yup"

He stopped and looked at me for a minute. He didn't say anything, just looked. "They" say when you're on an interview and the person interviewing you becomes silent, you should be silent also. It's usually this "silent time" that makes the interviewee uncomfortable and so they volunteer information to get rid of the silence, and they end up not getting the job. You wanna know why? Because they say something the Interviewer does not care to know. So I didn't say anything.

I could tell he was trying to go back to Cali on me, he just didn't know how to get there.

"So Kalico, do you still want to move to California?"

Damn! A direct flight. No layover in Dallas, nothing. He went straight to LAX. I gotta be honest now. 'Cause if I can't be honest with HIM, then I may as well not come back, right? I took a deep breath and told the truth.

# When Gucci Came First

"I use drugs and I drink a lot."
He didn't bat an eye. Why wasn't he surprised? He was supposed to be surprised. Did I look like a drug addict? Did I look like an alcoholic? Why wasn't he surprised?
"How much do you drink, Kalico?"
"What do you mean, how much do I drink?"
"One drink, three drinks?"
"No, four or five beers until I get almost drunk. A bottle or two of champagne, 'til I get tipsy."
"Do you smoke?"
"Cigarettes?"
"Whatever you smoke."
"Cigarettes, but only when I'm drunk or high."
"High?"
"Yes"
He didn't say anything, neither did I."
"Are you comfortable?"
"Right now?"
"Yes, Kalico."
"With you, this conversation or using drugs?"
"All"
"I'm comfortable."
"Why do you think you drink?"
"Because I'm not high."

Why was he focusing on my drinking? Weren't drugs worst than that?

"What kind of drugs do you use?"
"Coke. Cocaine, I know it's sad, isn't it?"
"Why do you say that?"
"Because I know better."
"You do?"
"Then, why do you do it, that's next, right?"
"If you want it to be."
"Isn't my time up?"
"Yes"

Saved. My fifty minutes were up. Time to go. I knew he wouldn't waste any time during my next session with those "how was your week" questions.

# MR. REALTOR

"Can I have forty dollars?"
"Here Kalico."

Everyday, my friend, Mr. Realtor would give me money.  He'd come to my job, take me out after work for drinks and something to eat and afterwards, I would stick my hand out and ask for money and go straight to Mt. Vernon where my package would be waiting for me.

At least I'm not spending my own money for this shit anymore.  Mr. Realtor was so good to me.  If I needed money for shopping, he was like "Here Kalico."  If I needed money for my hair (twice a week), he was like "Here Kalico."  And if it rained and I needed to go to the salon a third time, he was like, "Here Kalico."  My telephone bill was $390.00; he was like, "Here Kalico." This went on for over a year and I NEVER fucked him.  I kissed him twice.  And he would do anything for me and he proved it every single day. I really believed he loved me, but there was something about him I couldn't get with.  Something that wasn't right.  I didn't figure out what it was until we were walking down the street and he commented on two men.

"He's gay."
"How do you know?"
"Trust me, he's gay!"

I didn't say anything.  All I was interested in was my drinks, my food and the forty dollars I was going to ask him for.  We were going to Fridays near Grand Central Station.

"He's gay" he pointed to another man.
"How do you know?"

"Trust me, he's gay!"

# When Gucci Came First

The "gay" man walked by us.  I noticed they made eye contact.  What's this all about?  We entered Fridays.  Bubby was behind the bar.  He made my usual drink and gave Mr. Realtor a soda.  Mr. Realtor never drank, at least not in front of me anyway.  When my drink came, I ordered a Buffalo wing appetizer and my companion, Mr. Realtor ordered fried mushrooms.

Chomp.  Chomp.  Chomp.
Chomp.  Chomp.  Chomp.

Who was I eating with, Pac Man?  He chewed the food with his front teeth and held his lips tight.  It made me sick.  He even drank like that.  I brought it to his attention, in a loving way of course, but it was to no avail.

"I see I have to teach you table etiquette."
"My table manners are fine."
"I don't doubt that, I'm talking about the way you chew."
"What about the way I chew, Kalico?"

I showed him how he looked when he ate.  He thought it was funny. I could tell he was trying not to take it personal.  I suggested he chew his food toward the back of his mouth, something he claimed he already did.  Could have fooled me, I picked up my drink and took a sip.  Good, I could taste the liquor.

"How did you know those guys were gay?"
"I just did."
"How?"
"No Kalico, I'm not gay."
"How did you know I was going to go there?"
"'Cause I know you Kalico"
"No you don't, cause I wasn't even going to say that!"

I was lying.  I was going straight for the jugular.  If this nigga was gay, I wanted to know NOW!  I damn sure didn't want to find out after I gave him some pussy.  I know, my mouth is filthy.  Sorry.  But you see, my cousin was a telephone sex operator and she told me that eight out of ten men that called the line had fantasies of sucking another mans dick.

Deep right?  I also know two women who married faggots, sorry gay men (trying to be politically correct).  Nice looking men too…these women had children, purchased houses and then shortly after, learned of their husband's true sexual preference. The kickers to this shit was the two men, best friends for over twelve years, had a double wedding and everything, were fucking each other. Their wives thought they were joking at first. I damn sure was NOT going to give myself any first hand experiences to add to that story. Oh no, not me.

"But since you brought it up, I would like to know what makes you feel your opinion is expert to the point where you can detect someone's sexuality...do they give off some kind of scent like skunks?"

He was laughing really hard. Holding his stomach and everything. I know a lot of people say I should be a comedian, but I really wasn't trying to be funny this time.

"No gays don't give off a smell, you can just tell."

"How?"

"I can't explain it, you have to just know."

Well as Eddie Murphy would say, "that's a hint and a half for your ass!" What was Mr. Realtor trying to tell me? I didn't dwell on it and why the fuck should I, I'm 'getting too much money from him without fucking to care about whether or not he was a fruit loop. Not my problem, I finished my Buffalo wings and drink. Time to go.

"Can I have forty dollars?"

He pulled out a hundred-dollar bill to pay the waiter. After the tip Mr. Realtor had $61.00 left. I took fifty and left him with $11.00, just enough for him to get home and to the bank tomorrow.

# I ALWAYS FEEL LIKE SOMEBODY'S WATCHING ME

As soon as I got off the metro north, my "connect" was waiting for me. He would give me a kiss, a package and drive me to the bar I frequented. Everyday, the same routine.  In town by seven, high by seven thirty.

The bar was crowded.  It was Tuesday and everyone was out.  I sat in the middle of the bar and ordered champagne.  I had a "buzz" but wasn't high. I lit a cigarette.  The night was still young, so I decided I would try to make it home by midnight.  This girl walks over to me.
"Yo Kalico, you got anything?"

I turned around to see who the fuck would address me like that!

"I beg your pardon?"
"Do you have anything, I want a hit, but I don't want a full package, I'll give you five dollars."
"Nah, I don't have anything."

I picked up my drink and took a sip.  What in the fuck just happened?  I know this bitch didn't just ask me for cocaine, I barely knew her ass.  Where in the fuck did she get my business?  I finished my drink and called a taxi, time to go and it was only 10:40pm.

All I could think about was that chick asking me for a hit.  I was up 'til about four in the morning and I wasn't getting high.  I was thinking, something I hadn't done seriously in about a year.

Ring...ring...

Who in the hell is calling me this time of night, I picked up the phone.
"This better be Jesus or someone telling me they got the combination to the safe at Chase!"

# When Gucci Came First

"It's me Kalico, what are you doing?"
"Who is this?"

It was Mr. NBA wanting me to come to wherever he was.

"Nigga are you serious?"
"Who are you talking to, what's going on with you,  it's me."
"Fuck you, I know who it is, you got some nerve calling me after that bullshit you pulled with me in Asbury Park, you need to be thankful I didn't call the fuckin' cops and for the record, I've seen Mr. Nike commercial and he told me you videotaped that shit...well you can consider this advanced notice; if I ever find his statement has truth to it, I will be on the fucking news like all the rest of the women you have done shit to!"

I slammed the phone down and turned the ringer off.

In the morning there were three or four messages from Mr. NBA, yelling for me to pick up the phone and that he knows I didn't hang up on him. He wanted to know who I thought I was and if I forgot who he was.  He mentioned something about thinking that I loved him and oh I can't forget his "don't ever call me again, bitch" statement right before he hung up for the fourth time!

I downloaded the messages to a mini tape recorder given to me by a friend. Hmmm, I'll just keep this in my safe deposit box, you know...for SAFE keeping.

Don't ever call him again, please ... I don't recall calling him in the first place at 4 o'clock in the morning. He was truly lost, I guess that's one thing we both had in common...being lost and occasionally sleeping with members of the same sex. I guess that's two things depending upon how you view it.

# SESSION NO. 5 WITH THE THERAPIST

"Hello Kalico"
"Hi!"
"How are you today?"
"Okay, how are you?"
"Good, good"
"Kalico, last time we left off talking about your use of cocaine."
He paused, then continued… "Do you want me to refer you to a treatment facility?"
"No"
"It's just a suggestion"
"I know, but no thanks.  If I can't get myself off, then I don't deserve to be off."
"Why do you say that?"
"Well I don't recall needing anyone's help to get on drugs."
"Do you still want to move to California?"
"Yes"
"How would you get there?"
"Plane"
"Even though you think it may crash?"
"That's a chance I have to take."
"I see, so you like taking risks?"
"I guess, why else would I be doing drugs?"
"Why do you think you take risks?"
"Excitement!"
"Excitement?"
"Yes, just to prove I can do it and get away with it"
"Get away with it?"
"Yeah, do it and get over."
"Who are you proving yourself to?"
"Myself"
"Is that necessary?"

"Yes, for those watching."
"So you're proving something to people?"
"I guess"
"I see"
"It's like this, everyone thinks I'm a coke head now, family too – even though they haven't approached me on it.  And so by keeping myself up, while getting high, it's showing everyone, I'M NOT ADDICTED, I'm just having fun!"
"Keeping yourself up, what does that mean?"
"It means taking care of myself.  Continuing to buy new clothes, not getting skinny, keeping my apartment together.  You know, keeping myself up."
"Can you drive Kalico?"
"Yes"
"Do you have a license?"
"Yes, well actually it's a permit."
"If memory serves me correct, you can buy and insure a car with a permit."
"That's right"
"Do you own a car?"
"No"
"Why not?"
"I can't afford it."
"I see"

My fifty minutes were up.  Time to go.  I tried to analyze my session.  Was he trying to diss me?

I could afford a car if I wanted one, right?  Lord knows, I make enough money.  What was he getting at?  Was he trying to say I could have more if I stopped getting high?  It wasn't the car at all was it?  It was what the car SYMBOLIZED...

# I LOVE YOU TRULY...
# I LOVE YOU TRULY

Mr. Realtor took me out after work. This time we ate in Bryant Park. He ordered spring rolls, I had a glass of champagne and the house salad. We talked. We talked. I drank. I drank. I drank.

"Kalico, I love you."

"Is that song on the radio? 'Cause I've been hearing it a lot lately?"

I was dating Mr. Realtor and this African guy named Mohamed. I wasn't seriously interested in Mohamed and after Mr. Homosexual Detector made a habit of pointing out every man he thought was gay whenever we were out, I wasn't seriously interested in him either. He took my hand.

"I love you Kalico, and I want us to spend more time together."
"Yeah, yeah"
"I'm serious Kalico, you know I want to be engaged by mid 1999 and married shortly after."
"I know and YOU KNOW when I get married, I DON'T want to work, I want to go shopping every other week and I'm only having one kid!"
"I know"

Damn! I wish everything were that fuckin' easy.

"Can I have sixty dollars?"
"For what?"
"Don't ask me for what, just yes or no!"
"Okay, calm down."

I stuck my hand out. He hated that. He gave me sixty dollars.

"Make that seventy"

# WELL CONNECTED
# YOU CAN CHECK MY RECORD

He pulled out another ten.  It was time to go.  My connect was waiting for me at the train station in Mt. Vernon.  We walked to the Metro North.  I gave him a kiss on the cheek and boarded the train.  When I arrived in Mt. Vernon, my connect was still there waiting for me, I was forty minutes late.  He gave me a kiss, a package and dropped me to the bar.

"What's up Kalico Strong?"

That's what the owner of the bar calls me.

"What's up Tiny?"

Tiny is a good-looking man and I loved going to his place.  He always made me feel comfortable.  Translation: I could get drunk in his bar and not have to worry about anything.  He watched my back when I was too fucked up to watch it on my own.

Every night, one of the regulars would drop me off at home.  On several occasions, I damn near had to be carried up to my apartment, but no one every tried to "bother" me.  They would just drive me home and make sure I got upstairs safe.

"How was work Kalico?'
"Good, thanks"
"What you drinking?"
"Champagne split"

I had two and left.  I went home and took out my package, sniffed the entire thing and laid down.
My nose started running.

I took my hand and wiped my face, I looked.  Oh shit!  My nose was bleeding.

# When Gucci Came First

I jumped up and ran to the bathroom.  I wet a piece of tissue and stuck it up my nose.  It stung a little.  I was an official Coke Head!  Now my nose was damaged like this nigga I used to date from Yonkers.  I leaned my head back and started to pray.

"God please help me get off this shit.  Sorry I didn't mean to curse, no disrespect intended, but I'm scared.  God you know my heart, I'm really a nice girl, please help me before I experience something bad, thank you."

I took the tissue out of my nose and laid back down.

My nose stopped bleeding.

I wonder if I did any permanent damage to myself.  I'm not talking about the brain cells, memory loss or shit with my lungs and kidneys from smoking and drinking.  I was talking about my nose.  I wondered if the hair in my nose would grow back.  Does anyone know the answer to that?  If so, write me.

I decided to take a break from getting high and I was doing well until I arrived in Mt. Vernon.

"I'll just run to my grandmother's house, get my mail and get back on the train" that was the plan until I saw Denise.

"What's up Ho, why you ain't called me?"
"Denise, I've been busy."
"I know, I haven't seen you in a while, where you been?"
"Jersey"
"Well excuse me Big Time, I'm scared of you." She was funny like that.  I knew this conversation would lead to me getting high, but I would be smart this time and decline all offers. She continued, "Where you going?"
"To my grandmother's house right quick and then back to Jersey."
"To the projects, I'm walking that way."

We walked down Third Street towards Seventh Avenue.  Denise lived up the block from there.  When we got to my Grandmother's building she offered to come with me.  She wanted me to go with her home to have a couple of drinks and chat, since we hadn't seen each other in a while, I agreed.

As we got on the elevator, a woman was coming off and warned us to "watch out for the pee."

"Damn, I'll be glad when my Grandmother gets out of here!"
"Your Grandmother ain't going no where girl, shut up!"
"Just because she's set in her ways, doesn't mean she won't move if she had to, so you shut up!"

I knocked on my Grandmother's door.  I banged on the door.  My Grandmother wasn't home and I couldn't leave Mt. Vernon without my mail.  Shit, I guess I will have those few drinks Denise mentioned.

Twenty minutes into my visit with Denise, we were beeping my connect for a package.  Then another package and then another package…next thing I knew, it was two days later, I smelled like beer and aside from the twelve dollars it was going to take for me to get home, I was broke.

When Denise realized I didn't have any money left, her attitude changed. She was suddenly "tired" and "expecting her daughter" soon.  At that point, I did what she wanted me to…I left.

I never went back to visit Denise after that and I only saw her once.  Her front tooth was rotten and she had sores on her nose.  Two months ago I asked on of our old hang out partners about her, his response… "She's in the hospital."

# SESSION NO. 6 WITH THE THERAPIST

"Hey Doc"
"Hello Kalico, how are you today?"
"Great!"

I didn't ask him how he was doing.  I wanted to see if that would go unnoticed.
I wanted to see if he was paying attention.

"You don't want to know how I am?"
"Oh yeah, sorry, how are you doc?"  I smirked.
"Not so well"

Why was he telling me this?  Did I want to know?  Don't tell me my therapist
needed a therapist.  I know I'm not paying all this money for a fuckin' looser
doctor.  Oh I see, he wants to play "I'll take your place if you take mine" well
I'm very sorry, it isn't happening.

Now don't get me wrong, I like that game and I'm good at it, but this IS MY
fifty minute session, not his. So why is he fuckin' with me like this?  Does he
want me to react?  Of course he does, but in what capacity?  Shit!  I haven't
got time to be figuring out yet another motherfucker.  That's why I'm here
in the first place.  So busy figuring out people, I didn't have time to figure
out myself. I decided to indulge in a conversation with my therapist.  Maybe
this was part of my therapy.
"What's wrong doc?  Wanna talk about it?"

"My daughter has the pox"
"The Pox, what in the world is that?"
"Chicken Pox"
"And you want to be home with her?"

"Yes"

# When Gucci Came First

"So go home, I would like to think I'm not a code red."
"Code red?"
"Yeah, a dire situation."
"Are you getting along well Kalico?"
"As far as what?"
"Drinking and doing cocaine"
"Yeah, I guess I am"
"Have you done either since our last visit?"
"Yes"
"Which one?"
"Both"
"How many times?"
"Collectively?"
"No"
"I got high twice and I drank every day"
"Kalico, I know a wonderful…"
I cut him off before he could continue, "I'm not enrolling into any programs and I damn sure ain't going to no meetings!"
"I'm just worried about you Kalico"
"Aren't you going home to be with your daughter?"
"Kalico, I'm worried about you.  You are a beautiful young woman and very smart.  You have a lot of gifts, why do you want to die high?"
"What?"
"Can you tell the difference between boric acid and cocaine?"
"No"

His pager went off, "I have to go, Kalico please promise you won't get high before we speak again."

"Okay…Okay, I won't get high for the next seven days."

I put on my jacket.

"Is this twenty minute session free?"
"Yes it is Kalico, see you next week."

I shut the door behind me.



*The 1st Installment of the Kalico Jones Trilogy*

# IT'S HARD BEING THE FAMILY FOCUS

I have never seen so many envious family members in one unit in my life!  It gets to me sometimes like now.  I was just watching a basketball game with my mother and all she did was fuck with me, but I'm not surprised.  It's been that way since I've been at her house these past two weeks.  "Kalico this, Kalico fuckin' that!"  "Kalico I remember when you used to look like that, Kalico why can't you be with someone like this" or the "You know I heard you're bisexual" comment.  Time to fuckin' go.  She just signed my exit ticket, a week before Christmas.  I wish I could figure out what her fascination is with me.  I've had the best and I've seen the worst and when had, I gave.  And I still give now, even though I don't have as much.  My mother taught me just how quick niggas forget the good times.  I tried to overlook her pettiness, but pettiness is hard to overlook when it comes via a family member.  I guess 'cause that's what makes it hurt the most.

Mr. Realtor came by my job.  I suggested we go get something to eat.  We went to Bryant Park again where I handed him a gift bag.  He was shocked.

"Go ahead, open it."

He placed his hand in the bag and pulled out pair of black thong panties with a heart-shaped card that read:  "I think we should get to know each other better!"

He turned red.  I was smooth like that.  I needed him to help me and I didn't want sex to be an issue and the only way sex can be an issue between two people is if it isn't addressed.  Especially when the relationship is monetarily one sided.  GOD I HOPE MEN DON'T READ THIS BOOK!

The next couple of weeks after my infamous "panty note" you would have thought I hit the lotto.  I was shopping more, beauty salon three times a week, nails every other day, lobster and champagne…all at the expense of Mr. Realtor.  Life sure was good, but I knew that eventually I was going to have to either go to bed with Mr. Realtor or let him go.

You see, even though I was "in it for self" - I really cared for Mr. Realtor and despite my selfishness, I wanted him to be with someone who wanted to be with him, someone who wasn't a junkie. And besides that, I thought he was gay.

"I hate my job, I hate my job, I hate my job!" My daily morning chant. "I owe, I owe, so off to work I go!" My payday chant. Sad, but true. I would get to work at 8:45am and be fed up by 9:30am. Forty-five minutes is all it took. "God please don't let me leave here in handcuffs" my 9:45am chant and the "If assholes could fly, this place would be an airport" mid-day chant number two. If I weren't for these chants, I would have jumped up and slapped the shit out of somebody, because I really couldn't understand how some of the people I worked with got their jobs.

Shit...they were probably saying the same thing about me.

I just couldn't understand how anyone LIKED to work! I was smart enough to solve the Rubik's Cube and Chinese Arithmetic, but I couldn't figure out a way to convince myself the necessity of having a job. I took a three-week vacation. When I returned to work, I resigned from job number three.

You should have seen me when I walked out of there, I was smiling, singing, skipping and shit, all this with no job to fall back on, no money in the bank and a week later, no place to live. Who did I think I was, or better yet, what millionaire did I think I was related to?

Going from house to house without having money to eat is the most grounding experience anyone can have. You will come to your senses quick. Especially when you're in a situation where you can't go to anyone for help. This was MY situation. I ended up at my mother's house again. With her fucked up attitude, I knew my ass would find a job and an apartment in a hurry!

# SESSION NO. 7 WITH THE THERAPIST

"Good afternoon Doc, how's your daughter?"
"Fine, thanks…how are you Kalico?"
"Okay, but the question is how are you?"

Smiling, he explained how he and his wife had to put gloves on their daughter to keep her from scratching herself bloody.  YUCK! That was way more than my weak stomach cared to know.

"So Kalico, last time we spoke…I asked you to promise not to get high, did you?"
"No"
"Why not?"
"'Cause I promised."
"Is that the only reason?"
"Yeah"
"So if it's that simple, why not…"
I cut him off mid sentence and said, "Promise myself?"
"You got it"
"Because there's really nothing else I can do to make myself more disappointed in me."

He just looked at me.  Staring as though he couldn't believe what I was saying.

"Do you always speak so negatively about yourself?"
"No"
"Can you tell me something positive about yourself?"
"I'm creative"
"That's one"
"I'm fairly attractive."
"That's two"

"I'm a giver"
"I knew you could do it!"
"Ha, Ha, very funny!"
"So how's the job?"
"Great"
"Great, are we talking about the place from hell?  The if assholes could fly, this place would be an airport, place?"
"Yeah, I quit"

Maybe I shouldn't have told him that because of my insurance circumstance and all.

"How do you feel about your decision?"
"Good, I am now free of part of my problem."
"Problem?"
"Yeah, the drugs, the drinking, my attitude, all that has to come from somewhere."
"What makes up the other part?"
"Parts"
He repeated me, "Parts."
"Of the problem, right?"
"Yes, Kalico"
"My family relations, not really being able to say no, my reckless lifestyle, the abuse."

I didn't know how to slip that in, but the sexual abuse was something I needed to address.

"You think you were abused?"
"I was, by my babysitter and his brothers."
"Sexually?"
"Yes"

I could feel the tears coming to my eyes.  I decided to just let myself FEEL.

I cried the rest of the session.
"You don't have to talk about it if you don't want to."
"I was ten years old!  What is sexy about a ten-year-old?  What? What? What?"

I was now screaming.  I buried my head in my hands.  My therapist just let me cry.  I did just that.  Cried.  I was sure my fifty minutes were up, I stood up and headed for the door.

"Where are you going, Kalico?"
"My session is over."
"Don't worry about that, are you okay?"
"Yes"
"Kalico, I would like us to meet twice a week for a couple of weeks.  How do you feel about that?"
"Why, you think I'm crazy?"
"No, no why would I think that?  I just think that you and I should discuss what you've told me."
"Okay"
"See you in three days"

He helped me put on my jacket.

"Can I ask you a question?"
"Yes"
"And you will be honest?"
"Yes, Kalico"
"Do you think I can be saved?"
"You already are.  You save yourself every time you face your fears."

My session officially ended.  Time to go.

# EVERYBODY LOVES A STAR
# WHEN SHE'S ON THE TOP
# BUT NO ONE EVER COMES AROUND
# WHEN SHE STARTS TO DROP

And how the next month would prove that verse to be true.

Jackpot, Again!

This time, he was a Heavy Weight fighter.  Now I can't recall the exact way I met Mr. Professional Boxer and because this book is right and exact I have to leave that out, but don't worry…it won't affect the lesson.

Oh now I remember… I was at One Fish, Two Fish having dinner and drinks with these chicks from Harlem.

Ring…ring…ring…

My Grandmother's answering machine picked up.

"Please leave a message and I will get back to you" My Grandmother sounded like she was trying to get a record deal, singing on her machine with Barry White's "Practice what you preach" playing in the background.  I ran to hear who was leaving a message.

"Hello, this is Mr. Professional Boxer, please ask Kalico to…"

I picked up the telephone and in my "I was sleeping voice" said hello.  Now don't act like you don't know the fake sleep voice.  Ha ha ha.

"You were sleeping?"
"No"
"Oh, you sound like it."

# When Gucci Came First

"Actually I was reading." – **I was LYING!**
"Really?" he sounded shocked.

"Yes really, don't you?"
"Not often, but yes."
"So what's up gorgeous? I want to see you, let's go to dinner."
"Can we go for ice cream instead?"
"Why?"
"I just finished eating.  I cooked for me and my Grandmother" – **LYING!**
"What did you cook?"
"Baked chicken, macaroni and cheese and green beans…you should have called me earlier, I sent the rest over to my aunt's house"  - **STILL LYING!**
"Damn!"
"Unless you want me to cook you something right quick." – **FRONTING!**
"No baby, that's okay."
"Are you sure?"
"Yeah… Can I see you?  I'm on 241st Street."
"Of course"

I gave him directions.  He was less than ten minutes away.  I ran around my Grandmother's apartment grabbing lipstick and combs and the size six jeans from Ann Taylor that fit me oh so lovely.

I ran downstairs.  Eight fuckin' flights.  I didn't want him to see any other female, before he saw me.  I had no job and this man had money. He pulled up in a convertible sports car.  We drove to the other side of town and parked. We talked about his life, his baby's mother, his career, it was a relaxing change.

"So have you ever dated anyone is sports?"
"Yes"
"Who?"
"A basketball player"
"Who?"
"M#@#  (Mr. NBA's Name)."

You should have seen the look on his face.

"You know him?" I asked.

"Who DOESN'T know HIM?  He used to mess with one of my old

girlfriends."

He started the car.  Oh shit!  Dismissed before I got a chance.  In about three minutes we were back in front of my Grandmother's building, and by the time I put my hand on the door to open it, he was already out and on my side of the car opening the door for me.  As I got out, he gave me a hug and said, "You don't look like the type of young woman that would deal with him."

I didn't respond.  I just walked in the building.  I never heard from him again.

A few weeks later, I watched him fight on cable.  I fell asleep before it was over.  I haven't heard anything about him.  His fights are still not of the Roy Jones / Mike Tyson caliber, but I hear he's doing okay for himself.

After that experience with Mr. Professional Boxer, I vowed never to speak of Mr. NBA to any perspective male associations.  It wasn't worth the loss potential.

Looking back on Mr. Boxer, I wondered what he meant by what would be his final words to me.  I guess I'll never know.

# EVERYBODY'S TALKING
# ALL THIS STUFF ABOUT ME
# WHY CAN'T THEY JUST LET ME LIVE?

In the meantime word of my so-called "drug abuse" spread through Mt. Vernon like fire. I didn't know what the "inside word" was about me and probably would have never known if it weren't for an enemy. Yes, I said enemy. I was sitting at the bar of a local hang out, my nails weren't done and my hair was on day eight, when she sat down next to me.

Sarcastically and without wasting any time, she said, "Kalico, I know we don't speak, but..."
I cut her right off and without even turning around to face her I said, "and we wont."
"Look you don't have to get smart with me, I'm just..."
"Being nosey! And don't get smart with you? Please...I know you called my name and shit, but it's obvious you don't know me. And lets face it, you're only speaking to me to fuck with me and I'm not in the mood, so don't waste your time!"
"I'm not trying to get on your bad side, I just want to ask you a question."
I sucked my teeth, "What is it?"
"Why are you giving the streets something to focus on?"

She got up and walked away. I looked at my undone nails, eight-day hair and nearly blood shot eyes in the mirror behind the bar, and I called a taxi.
I thought about what my enemy had said to me all night. I wondered in what capacity her statement was intended. I figured it out. I packed my shit, called my cousin Mike and left Mt. Vernon that night. My enemy ended up being my friend that night in the bar and although she and I don't speak to this day, I knew that she did care about me in some weird kind of way.

Do not give the streets anything to focus on!
Do not give the streets anything to focus on!

# When Gucci Came First

Do not give the streets anything to focus on!
Do not give the streets anything to focus on!
Do not give the streets anything to focus on!
Do not give the streets anything to focus on!
Do not give the streets anything to focus on!

# MONTCLAIR, NJ 07042

The Palm Grill Bar and Restaurant, Montclair – New Jersey, that's where I met Susan. We hit it off immediately.

"So Kalico, you live in Montclair?"
"Yes"
"Always?"
"No, I moved here from Mt. Vernon."
"Where?"
"Westchester"
"Oh, upstate New York."

I smiled. Thank goodness she got it right. It's hell trying to explain where Mt. Vernon is to people outside of New York.

"You have a nice smile."

Yeah, that's what she SAID, but I knew what she really MEANT. She wanted to have sex with me. I was in the mood too. Not so much for sex, but for affection. There IS a difference you know. I gave her the eye contact she wanted. The eye contact that would let her know I was with WHATEVER she was with. I smiled again and said, "Thank you." I took a sip of my drink.

It was unspoken, but official. Susan and I were going to have sex.

"This place is boring."
"Yeah, I know"
"You wanna come over, I only live a few blocks away?"

I hesitated and she insisted. I was reluctant, she was persistent. She grabbed her jacket and walked towards the door. I pulled my coat off the back of the barstool and followed. We took her car. 12:15am.

# When Gucci Came First

"So Kalico, Hmmm."
"What's the Hmmm for?"
"Do you, oh forget it."
"No, what is it?"
"Nothing. Well, here we are."

Damn! This chick had paper (money)! The front of the house was complete with a fuckin' waterfall. She had what appeared to be Palm trees lining her drive way, and there were enough cars in front of the house to put on a mini car show. Trying not to appear IMPRESSED, I kept my mouth shut and followed her into the house.

You could tell she was used to the best of everything. Her viewing room television was the biggest thing I've ever seen outside of an actual movie theater. When I asked Susan what the size of her TV was, she responded, "Oh, I don't know, the size of the wall I guess." And she wasn't trying to be funny either, that's just how she was about her house. She was just so used to having, that the size of her television was a minor thing to her. She took me on a tour of her house, basement included, before we settled on the plush white sofa in her guest living room.

"Get comfortable, take your shoes off."

I did.

"Are you okay with this?"
"With what? Being here or being here with you?"
"You're very very, what's the word I'm looking for?"
"Uhhh, I don't know…upfront, maybe."

She said nothing. She pulled out a cellophane bag and sat back on the sofa. She put her nail in the bag and into her left nostril. Damn! Why can't I get away from this shit? Every time I turn around, coke, coke, and more coke. Ever since my ass started sniffing, it seems like I only meet "sniffers" or "closet crack heads." I was starting to wonder if I knew anyone who WASN'T a fuckin' junkie.

Susan sat up and passed the bag to me.

"How do you know I do this?"
"Do you?"

# When Gucci Came First

"Yeah"
"Well then, that question is irrelevant!"

I took a couple of hits and cracked open a beer. I sat back on the sofa and sized up my host. Nice teeth…beautiful hair…Great breasts (she said she got "them" for Christmas)… shapely mid section and pretty feet, no wonder she had it all, anyone would be more than happy to take care of her. I know she didn't have a hard time obtaining anything she really wanted, and tonight would be no different for Susan, 'cause she sure as hell could have me, if she wanted. She slid over towards me and put her head on my shoulder and rubbed her lips against my neck. I could tell she wanted something from me, just as I wanted something from her. I don't think it was that we wanted each other. I think we just wanted to feel something. Something that was missing in our lives, the same something that had us both on her sofa.

I wondered how could something so MISSING be so PRESENT?

A DEEP thought for you?

We started kissing and rubbing each other's breast. She stood up and took my hand, she was
leading me to her bedroom. We undressed each other, and fell on the bed. I rolled my tongue over her breasts, she rolled her tongue down my stomach, she played with my hair, and I turned her over on her back. We had sex, the feeling was intense, and Susan…she was insatiable, she was gorgeous and…

She was WHITE!

Afterwards we just laid there, enjoying the remnants of what we just accomplished. She leaned over and kissed me. My high was over and reality was rearing it's ugly head. It was time to go. I looked at my watch, it was almost three in the morning.

# SESSION NO. 8 WITH THE THERAPIST

"Hello Kalico"
"What's up?"
"How are you?"
"Okay, how are you?"
"Good, good"
"I got high the other day"
"And?"
"I felt bad"
"Good"
"Good"
"Good"
"Why is that good?"
"Because when you regret your actions, you are less likely to repeat them."
"Really?"
"Yes"
"I hope you're right"
"Kalico, you mentioned that you were abused by your baby sitters, how have you been dealing with that?"
"I've been okay.  I thought about it a couple of times, but I feel better now that I got it out in the open."
"In the open?"
"Yeah…you know verbally…actually saying it to someone aloud."
"You never told anyone Kalico?"
"No"
"Why?"
"I was ashamed"
"Of what THEY had done to YOU?"
"Yes"

My therapist changed the topic.  Why I don't know.  Maybe he thought we uncovered enough information in regard to that subject for now.  He looked at me and smiled.

# When Gucci Came First

"What about cocaine?"
"What about it?"
"Have you been getting high?"
"I told you I did and how I felt bad about it, when I walked in… remember?"
"Yes, do you still feel bad about it?"
"Of course, so stop asking me that, okay?"
"Okay"

I felt myself going into bitch mode. Is he a quack? Is there some place he'd rather be? 'Cause if it is, end the session and let my ass go, Lord knows I don't wanna be holding nobody up! And if he is gonna be here, then the least he could do is HIS JOB and remember the fuckin' facts.

"What's worst for you the sexual abuse by your baby sitters or you being addicted to drugs?"
No he didn't. First off… BOTH of those were rotten situations, but the second situation was of no meaning to me, because for one, I WASN'T addicted – I was a SOCIAL engager and two, it wasn't drugs – plural – it was DRUG – singular -ONE DRUG - COCAINE! Was he purposely trying to see if he could get me to go the fuck off? I answered, "The abuse."
"Why Kalico?"
"Because I think the abuse I suffered growing up contributed to my current situation."
"What situation is that?"

I looked at my watch. It sure would be nice if this session was over, but unfortunately I had four minutes left.

"The drug abuse, the narcissistic slash exhibitionist slash introvert mood swings due to a severe lack of self esteem." You go girl! Now who sounded like they were sitting BEHIND the desk?
"Kalico, please do not get high."
"Okay"

He shook my hand. My fifty minutes were up. Time to go.

# THE FREAKS COME OUT AT NIGHT

Susan called me all week.  We met for lunch twice and tonight, we were meeting at the Palm Grill.  We were going to have drinks, then go back to her place, that was the plan until she told me she had to cook food for a sick relative.  I wanted to postpone in lieu of her Aunt's illness, but she insisted I come straight to her house.  She said we would have a few drinks indoors. I agreed.  I rang the doorbell and Susan (lets just refer to her as Mrs. White from here on), opened the door wearing this itty-bitty halter-top and panties. I said hello and walked into the guest living.  I made myself comfortable.  She sat next to me.

"How ya doing?"
"Fine and yourself?"  I was starring at her breasts.
"Better now"

She leaned over and kissed me.  Her lips were soft. She was still preparing dinner.  She got up and went back in the kitchen, but not before handing me a folded twenty-dollar bill filled with cocaine.  I put it on the table.  I looked at it for about ten minutes arguing with myself about why just one sniff wouldn't hurt me.  I was high seven minutes later.

Five minutes after that, Mrs. White finished cooking.  Ten minutes after that we were on the floor having sex, when we heard the door unlock.

It was too late for us to get up or dressed, It happened too fast for us to even get a story straight!  I looked at Mrs. White, she must have seen the fear and embarrassment in my eyes, because she grabbed my hand and squeezed it in a kind of like "we're in this together" way and with her other hand, she caressed my breasts.  Was this bitch crazy?  Doesn't she realize someone is entering her house?  I removed her hand from my breasts.  She began to kiss me.  I was confused, I grabbed her face and whispered, "Someone is coming, stop"
She leaned over and whispered back, "I know, it's my husband."

     *The 1st Installment of the Kalico Jones Trilogy*

# When Gucci Came First

Well I'll be damn, she really was crazy. She didn't even stop. She just kept mumbling something about being horny. I personally, was out of the mood.

"Relax, he knows I like women, he's okay with it."

I couldn't respond. How do you begin to respond to some thing like this? What was I supposed to say, "oh really" or I know…I know…how about this one… "Wanna do a threesome?" Too late, he was already standing over us.

I was speechless. I recognized him. He had been a musical guest on Saturday Night live. I think he knew I recognized him, who wouldn't.

I needed another beer.

"Hi, you must be Kalico, I'm Mr. White"

Just like that. No, "bitch what are you doing with my wife!" No "Please get your shit together and go." Nothing. He said hello and walked past us and into the bathroom. Mrs. White got up and followed.

I got up and made an attempt to locate my bra and panties. Here are the panties, where in the fuck did she throw my bra? Fuck it, it's left. I have millions of them anyway. I put leg one in my pants. Mrs. White came out of the bathroom.

"Whatcha doing?"
"Getting dressed"
"Why?"
"What do you mean why? Your husband is home!"
"So, I want you again"

She was kissing my inner thigh, while I was trying to pull up my pants. She started licking me. I leaned back and thought to myself, "If he's okay with it, then fuck it!" I let her do what she wanted. He came out of the bathroom and watched.

Buzzzzz Buzzzzzzzzz, next thing I know, Mr. White was waving a vibrator. He wanted to join in. I was high, drunk and horny. Mrs. White insisted and I went along with it. I couldn't believe she was asking me to have sex with her husband and right in front of her too. She was sucking my breasts and her husband was fingering me.  I couldn't believe it.  Then he was sucking my breasts and she was licking my pussy (I hate that word).  The episode we swung was truly rated X.

**3:57am**

My high was coming down and reality was setting in.  I wanted to go home.  They insisted on driving me, I declined the offer and called a taxi.  I wanted to be alone.  I wanted to think.

What am I going through?  What is making me do these things?  What is it about me that attracts people of this nature?  I couldn't answer my own questions.  It was three weeks before I returned any of Mrs. White's calls.

Ring…ring…
"Hi, no one is home to take your call at the moment."

It was Mr. and Mrs. White's answering machine.  Good!  I didn't want to speak with them anyway.  What would I say, "Hi, it was great fucking you and your husband" and I didn't want to have to answer the "when can we do it again" question,  So this is what I came up with: "Hey, this is Kalico – returning your call.  I hope everything is well, bye."

Whew!  That was easy.  They weren't home.  I wish life was this easy all the time. I turned out the light and just as my head hit the pillow, my phone rang.  Should I answer it?  It CAN'T be Mr. and Mrs. White, they're not home.  And if it is, I am a grown woman and therefore don't have to participate in anything that I don't want to participate in, right?  So why was I contemplating whether or not I should answer my own damn phone?  I picked it up.

"Hello"
"Hey Kalico,  it's Mrs. White!"

Shit!

"We were screening calls and you hung up before we could turn the machine off."
"Oh well, what's up?"
"Nothing, we were just wondering what you've been up to."
"Working, shopping, the usual"

# When Gucci Came First

"Oh because we hadn't heard from you."
"Oh"
"Is everything alright?"
"Yeah, why do you ask?"
"You seem a little down"
"I'm okay"
"Wanna come over?  We'll cheer you up!"
"I'm not dressed and I have to get up early in the morning."
"Mr. White is on his way, we'll get you home early."

She hung up.

Damn!  How can I not go now?  And did you notice all the WE words being used?  We were now THREE.  I ran around my apartment like a chicken with it's head cut off, searching for something to wear.  I hadn't washed clothes in a month.  So black spandex, boots and a multi colored short sleeve shirt were my only option.  My bell rang.  Damn!  Did he speed?  And if so, why?  Was I the entertainment for the night?  I decided to skip the ritual that is called make-up, I grabbed a jacket.

When I got downstairs, Mr. White was parked directly in front of my building in a beat up pick-up truck.  My nosey ass superintendent was outside staring.  She made it a point to speak to me.

"Hi Kalico"
"Hey"
"Going out?"
"No"

No bitch, I'm NOT going out.  I'm just outside, fully dressed, getting into a goddamn ride.  Why are you wasting my time with this dumb ass question?  When you're really trying to figure out what I'm doing with this white man!  Nosey bitch!  I got in the pick-up disgusted.  Is this an example of what my life would be?

"Hey Mr. White."

"Hi Kalico, I'm just going to make a quick stop before we head to the house, is that okay with you?"

Like I was going to say no.  Don't you just hate it when people ask you questions when there really is only one answer?  Why bother?  I mean,  it's not like you really have other options to choose from.

"No I don't mind"

I didn't say shit else for the rest of the ride.  He kept trying to initiate conversation, but it didn't work.  I kept my responses to one or two words. I didn't know what was in store for me courtesy of my newfound friends, but whatever it was, I damn sure ain't contributing to  it's development.  We arrived at their house.  Mrs. White greeted us at the door, half dressed – as usual.  She gave me a hug and took my jacket.  Mr. White pulled out little glass bottles of cocaine from his pants pocket and emptied them into a dish. I made myself a drink.  We were all sitting on the sofa.

"You know Kalico, we're so happy to have met you."
"I'm happy to know you guys as well"

Mr. White interjected, "No, I don't think you understand, we've put ads in the paper for a black girl, we were even willing to pay!"

No this bitch didn't set me up!  I tried not to appear affected by what was just said to me.  I looked at Mrs. White. I was trying to figure out what to say to her, but I guess my brain didn't relay the "don't appear affected" message to my face, 'cause Mr. White turned to his wife and said, "You didn't tell her?" - Mrs. White didn't say anything.

I couldn't believe it…this bitch set me up and did he just mention possible payment?  Now they were talking my language.  You set me up so you wouldn't have to pay me?  Is this what the drinks are about?  Is this where the cocaine comes into play?  Oh now I see. Well I'm not sniffing or fucking until we establish an economically feasible payment arrangement and I wanted my money BWB (before we begin), on a projected hourly rate.

# I'M ALWAYS A BUSINESSWOMAN FIRST! A WHORE SECOND, DON'T GET IT TWISTED!

Mrs. White handed me a dollar bill filled with cocaine.

"No thanks."

I gave it back to her with the "I'm disappointed in you" look. She knew she fucked up even though none of us acknowledged it verbally. Surprised by my declination, she said, "are you sure?"

What the hell, I took a few hits and promised myself that I would remain fully clothed, multi-colored short sleeve summer shirt and all. That'll teach her a lesson.

By the end of the night we had come to an agreement on my fee. $300.00 an hour. Mr. White asked if I could hang out with them tonight and be paid on Thursday. Sorry no credit. I'm sure you understand this is now business. He agreed. See ya Thursday, I called a taxi. During the ride home, I realized how totally turned off I was when it came to Mrs. White. She did nothing for my libido, but her husband's paycheck, now THAT got my juices flowing.

I decided to skip my therapy appointment. I didn't feel up for the dramatics. My mind was focused on my $300 an hour financial arrangement with the white couple, as I truly felt I was doing something new. I even thought Mr. and Mrs. White were doing something new. As it turns out, they weren't.


**Thursday. 8:30 p.m.**

I arrived at Mr. and Mrs. White's house ready to rumble (for my previously agreed upon hourly rate of 300 BWB – of course).

# When Gucci Came First

I walked in.

Mrs. White directed me straight to the bedroom where her husband was waiting with two dildos, a vibrator that looked bigger than the last one, and an X-rated movie already playing in the VCR.

I looked around the room.

There were handcuffs, a blindfold and three black candles at each corner of the bed.  I heard a slam!  I turned around…Mrs. White had closed the bedroom door and locked it.  She was dressed in a black leather outfit with a mask.

I turned towards her husband.

He was motioning me to sit down on the bed.

I did.

They undressed me and wrapped me in a white terry cloth robe with a hood.  What the fuck did my black ass stumble upon?  I looked at the television, these motherfuckers were watching an S&M video.  Oh shit!  Was I getting ready to be sacrificed?  My heart was beating so hard and so fast that I could actually see it pushing through my chest.  I began to pray.  "God please let me live through this, I promise I won't get high again!"  I opened my eyes.  Mrs. White was licking my clitoris, while her husband masturbated.  He made himself come.  He was screaming and shaking and everything.  He then grabbed one of the candles from the corner of the bed and began to let the hot wax drip on his neck, then his chest, then his penis.  He was getting hard again and he wasn't even touching himself.  Mrs. White stopped licking me and crawled over me towards her husband.  She grabbed a candle.  What was this bitch about to do?  I hope she wasn't thinking about pouring that shit on my ass.  She lifted the candle over her head and leaned back.  I watched, as the hot wax spilled onto her breasts.  She massaged the shit in until the wax hardened.  She then took the candle and inserted in her vagina, but not the end that was lit, but so fuckin' what.  This couple was CRAZY!  I have to get the hell out of here.  I had twenty minutes to go if I wanted my money.  Shit!  I prayed again.  "God please get me outta here safe, I will never come back."

Just then Mrs. White handed me a candle.  She asked me to drip wax on her

                     *The 1st Installment of the Kalico Jones Trilogy*

# When Gucci Came First

husband's nipples.  I did.  She asked me to drip wax on his stomach.  I did.  She asked me to drip wax on his penis.  I did.  She turned her husband over and whispered for me to stick the candle in his ass.  Now I KNOW she didn't just say, what I THINK she said.  I couldn't have possibly heard her correctly.  Stick what...where?  She said it again. And with a puzzled look on my face, I leaned over the Mr. White for some kind of emotion, something to let my black ass know he was not co-signing this shit his wife just asked me to do when, Mrs. White took my hand and guided me toward her husbands butt... she was actually attempting to assist me in fulfilling this sick ass request.  My hand was shaking to the point where the candle wasn't steady, I'm thinking, "damn, this is about to be a situation if this candle gets stuck." Mrs. White is gently rubbing my back while this is going down, how in the hell could she watch this shit?  How could she watch someone stick a candlestick up her husband's ass?  Was this the reason they couldn't find a third party for their bedroom?  I bet it was, freaky asses.  I took a deep breath and did it.  I put that candlestick right up Mr. White's ass.  He let out a scream,  I looked at his wife.  She was fingering herself.  I tapped her on the shoulder and without waiting for my question, she said, "He's okay, you excited him, do it again."  She gave me a small plastic bottle of baby oil.

"Squirt this on his toushy while you put in and out" – she instructed.  I looked at the clock. I had thirteen minutes to go.  Why is it that every time you're doing something you don't want to do, time goes slow?  If anyone should figure that out, please write me.

$300.00 an hour with a few minutes to go.  I looked at the candle, took a deep breath and did what I was told.

In...out...squirt...squirt...in  ...out...squirt...squirt... in... out...squirt... squirt...in...out...squirt...squirt...in...out...

And he was loving it.  Twisting, turning, screaming and then he yelled, "Harder!"

Oh hell no!  See this is where I draw the line folks.  I glanced at Mrs. White, she was screaming "Harder" too.  As though I was sticking the candle up her ass, "He's about to come" she yelled.  He turned over on his back and lifted his legs so that I could continue with the candlestick. I did just that, in...out...squirt...squirt...in...out... and next thing I know, Mr. AND Mrs. White are screaming at the top of their lungs, it was crazy, I couldn't believe my eyes, "I'm coming, you coming, I'm coming, you coming!" back and

# When Gucci Came First

forth to each other.  Mrs. White at one end of the bed with a finger in her p@#$@, sucking on her breast and Mr. White at the other end of the bed with a candlestick up his ass, drenched in baby oil.  A few moments later, they came.  Semen shot straight from his penis, almost touching the ceiling.  Mrs. White had sweat pouring off her as if she had just ran the New York Marathon and me, if memory serves me correct, I was now owed $300.00 and I didn't even have to use my "personal."  I took off the robe and gathered my clothes.  Now dressed and ready to go, I called a taxi.  Mr. and Mrs. White Couple were now having sex.  When I heard the taxi horn, I politely entered their bedroom and asked to be paid.

"Uh, uh, excuse me…the taxi is outside."

I got no response.

"Umm excuse me, Mr. and Mrs. White Couple, I hate to be rude, but my cab is outside and I…"
Mr. White responded, "It's on top of the television Kalico, thanks and please make sure you lock the door when you leave."

I guess they weren't going to stop to say goodbye.  I located my envelope on top of the TV and closed the door behind me.  I made sure the front door was secure.

And got in the taxi.

I opened the envelope, there was a note and $400.00 in it.  I read the letter:

*"Thanks for being a good sport, enjoy the money… this was a fantasy.  Take care of yourself kiddo!"*

What!  No I didn't just get played.  I sat up all night thinking about that shit.  I don't know why my feelings were hurt, but they were.

Now I know how tissue feels.

Used, discarded and forgotten.

I made a cocaine call.  I wasn't going to sleep at this point anyway and I did have an extra hundred dollars.  So that's like found money, right?  I waited two hours.  My NJ connect never called back. I woke up with $400.00 in my pocket the next day.  I was glad he didn't call me back.

# SESSION NO. 9 WITH THE THERAPIST

"Hello Kalico"

"Hi"

"Haven't seen you in a while" I didn't even entertain that statement.  He continued. "How have you been?"

"Good"

"Good, glad to hear it."

I was not in the mood for this psycho dramatic bullshit today.  I had a bunch of things on my mind and this fifty-minute session wasn't one of them.  I felt the bitch mode switch about to be tampered with.

"I want to go back to one weekly session"

"Why?"

"Because this is a lot of traveling" Damn that sounded stupid, but I couldn't think of anything else to say.

"You live in New Jersey now, right?"

"Yeah, with my mother."

"Are you having problems at home?"

"No"

"You don't like living with your mother?"

"Hate it"

"Why?"

"She doesn't understand me, I think she's just as happy as the rest of my enemies right now."

"Happy about what?"

"Happy that I'm all fucked up to the point where I had to give up my apartment and of course, the drug and alcohol thing too."

"Why?"

"Trust me, she's happy"

"Why would your mother be happy about your unhappiness?"

"'Cause she never liked me and maybe she wishes she could do what I do, you know when she was my age."

# When Gucci Came First

"Jealousy?"

"Maybe," I continued... "And it's a damn shame, but I truly wish I could just say fuck everybody and get on a plane and go!"

"Why?"

"'Cause she's always reminding me that I have no place to live now and she's rude for no reason and sarcastic and above all, she seems to have forgotten all the nice things I have done for her, when my brothers...fuck it, this is not about them."

I was now crying. He handed me a small box of tissue.

"Are you okay Kalico?"

"Yes"

"Do you want to continue?"

"Yes"

"Are you upset that she doesn't acknowledge the good things?"

"She never did. Everything is always negative. My clothes, my friends, me being sick."

"You're sick?"

"Yes, and I've been taking medication for a few months. I was in and out of the emergency room all summer. I couldn't work. I was sleeping sometimes twenty hours a day. I lost weight and my job did could not give me disability because I wasn't there long enough. I was behind in all my bills, including rent. At one point, I was on five different medications, including a steroid. I was weak and because I wasn't getting assistance, I had no food in my house. She didn't even care. That was fucked up."

"Did you explain this to your mother?"

"I should not have had to, she knew."

"Did you tell her?"

"No"

"Then how do you know she was aware?"

I didn't respond.

"Kalico, I don't think your mom or any mom would let their sick child go without food."

He obviously didn't know my mother. And who's side was he on anyway? How could he say that to me? Who made him my family's dysfunction justifier? Was he at the every weekend cookouts I threw for my family? Was he at the store when I purchased not one, but two pools for our enjoyment complete with water guns and pool toys?  Oh I got it, he was one of the cashiers at Path Mark who rang up well over 300 dollars worth of steak, seafood, etc. to feed seven people with expensive taste No I don't recall seeing him around.   And the way I was feeling, this session has been over! I'm just waiting for my fifty minutes to expire.

"You don't know my mother, and until you meet her and see us interact, your opinion is based in ignorance!"

FLICK! The bitch mode switch was activated.

My therapist just sat there for a moment with a blank look on his face, what was he thinking?  Did I make him mad?  Did he want me to leave?  What?

"Okay Kalico, you're right…would you like your mom to attend one of your sessions?"
"No"
"Why not? Maybe it will be good for you."
"Or maybe it will be good for her."
"Why would it be good for her and not you, Kalico?"
"Because this will be another thing she could be happy about."
"Happy about?"
"Yeah happy that on top of all the other shit I'm going through, I don't even have enough will power or love for myself to help myself.  Happy that I now have to meet with someone to tell me about me – like you would know me better than I know myself, and we both know that ain't true… my mother would be ecstatic!"
"Think about it."
"I said no!"
"Okay, but I do family counseling also."

My fifty minutes were up.  Time to go.  As I grabbed my coat and headed for the door, I turned to Dr. Weintraub (not his real name, so

forget about it)and said, "It's not that I want her to say Thank you or even treat me like I treat her, but it would be nice to feel like she loved me and not because she gave birth to me, but because I'm a great person and I'm loveable."
I felt the tears coming, I grabbed a few tissues off his desk and left.

I needed money. My grandmother's phone bill was $389.00 where in the fuck was I getting that?  I called Mr. Realtor.

# HERE I COME TO SAVE THE DAY!

Ring…ring…ring…

"Hello Kalico."
"How did you know it was me?"
"Caller I.D., you're not at work, why?"
"Don't question me, I hate that!"
"Calm down, what' s up?"
"I need you."
"How much?"

I started laughing. One thing about my relationship with Mr. Realtor, he knew I wanted money 90 percent of the time, so I didn't have to front and he didn't either.

"$400.00"
"For what?"
"My phone bill, you can give me a money order made out to Bell Atlantic"
"When do you need it?"
"As soon as possible."
"Tomorrow?"
"Yes, can you bring it to Mt. Vernon?"
"Okay"
"Thank you."
"Where are you going now?"
"No where, I'm reading the job section of the NY Times."
"Don't quit your job Kalico."
"Okay, okay."
"I gotta go, I'll bring you the money tomorrow."
"Bye" I hung up.

What a load off me.  Mr. Realtor to the rescue, yet again.  I know he was tired of me, he just didn't know how to break free.  A lot of men had that problem

# When Gucci Came First

when it came to me.  I guess I used what was done to me, on them.  Mental entrapment & Material enslavement, but in a different form:

**POTENTIAL FUTURE PUSSY ENTRAPMENT AND EMOTIONAL ENSLAVEMENT.  YOU GIVE ME TODAY, BASED ON WHAT YOU THINK I'M GOING TO GIVE YOU TOMORROW.**

Simple, but there was only one way you could obtain the kind of game I had…

You had to be abused.
Unfortunately I applied my "game" to people who didn't deserve to be mistreated or deceived.  But like a cancer, I couldn't stop it.  I could only slow it down for while.  That's it.

I met Mr. Realtor at the Metro North train station.  We went to dinner.  He gave me the money order and $50.00.  I walked him back to the train. It was cold.  I thought about him all night.  I knew we couldn't be together, but how could I break off this "thing" without hurting him?  I thought of something.

On my way home, I stopped by the local bar.

"Kalico Strong"
"What's up Tiny?"
"Champagne?"
 "Yup"

The bar was crowded for a Wednesday.  I had a couple of drinks and thought of my decision to end it with Mr. Realtor.  My cellular phone rang.

"Hello"
"What's up bitch?"
"Who is this?"
"Naomi bitch, what ya doing?"

"Hey Ni!"

Naomi is my friend from Cali.  Hanunah Sabur.  She was up for a few weeks last November.  We keep in touch.

# When Gucci Came First

"Whatcha doin' it's hella noisy?"
"I'm having a drink."
"You at a bar bitch?"
"Yeah"
"Well I'm coming your way."
"When?"
"Soon"

I heard her drop the phone. She was cursing at someone. She's crazy like that. She returned to the phone.

"I gotta go, this motherfucker almost hit my car and there's a sale at Gucci, I'll call you later. I love you Bitch!"
"I love you too, be easy!"

I miss Naomi. I went into the bathroom and said a prayer, "God, please watch over my friend, thank you." I came out and finished drink number four.

**Two hours later...**

"Who's gonna give me a ride home?" I yelled. "Who's gonna give me a ride home?" Again, I yelled... this time louder and spitting all over the place.
"Alright, who's taking Kalico home?" – Tiny yelled over the noisy crowd and music.
"I will" it was my friend, Mr. Car Dealer.
"Are you ready?"
"Yes"

He helped me put on my jacket. As I was walking out of the bar (with Mr. Car Dealer's assistance), I saw my connect. He asked if I was okay getting home, I said yes and proceeded out the door. I didn't feel like getting high.

I don't remember anything between the time I saw my connect as I walked out the bar and waking up the next morning with my clothes on and the heel on my left boot being completely off. I guess I was too drunk.

I decided not to go to work.

All I thought about for the next couple of days was Mr. and Mrs. White Couple. I still couldn't get over the way I felt I got played. I picked up the



*The 1st Installment of the Kalico Jones Trilogy*

phone and dialed their number.  I figured I'd do a "Hi, I'm moving call" or something to that effect.  Anything to get closure, anything to stroke my ego.  Maybe they tried to reach me after that and couldn't, after all… I did move.

(973) 509 ----

Ring…

"I'm sorry the number you have reached has been changed to a non-published number."

Oh shit!  I really felt like a piece of tissue now.  I should have left well enough alone. I wish I never called.

I never saw Susan or Ricky again.

# A HARD HEAD MAKES A SOFT ASS

So I've been told.  I just couldn't understand why I always had to learn the hard way.  Why I kept traveling down the same exact path, EVERY TIME. I couldn't figure out a way to stop myself.  It was like, okay Kalico you DO see the brick wall ahead, right?  And I'd be like yes, I see the wall and then I would step on the gas.  100 miles per hour, headed straight for the wall, saying to myself, well maybe it really ISNT a brick wall this time, maybe it's a hologram?  I love a risk.  I just hope they don't kill me.

How in the world was I going to break up with Mr. Realtor?  I knew I had to do it, but how?  I know…I'll do a T. Banks and leave a message on his answering machine.  Nah, that ain't right, I'll write him a letter.  I'm good at writing letters – it read something like this:

*Dear Mr. Realtor:*

*We've known each other for a couple of years now and although I know you know what I ultimately want out of a relationship, I don't see us going in that direction.  Aside from going out after work, I don't see you.  I have no idea what you do after I leave you to go home, and you have yet to invite me to your home or out on the weekend.  It's like you just give me money to keep me from asking you questions or keep you from having to spend time with me.* ***(TRYING TO MAKE HIM FEEL AS THOUGH HE'S THE REASON FOR THE BREAK UP, DIDN'T GIVE A SHIT ABOUT WHAT HE DID AFTER HE TOOK ME FOR DRINKS AND GAVE ME MY DAILY ALLOWANCE).*** *I have tried several times to get you to be more assertive and aggressive with me and within our relationship, but it has been to no avail.  I feel as though we are only buddies. Maybe you really don't want to participate in this thing with me any longer and just don't know how to say it.  We aren't even having sex!  I think we've known each other long enough to be beyond this point.* ***(HAD NO INTENTION OF EVER FUCKING HIM, EVER, EVER, EVER, BUT I WANTED HIM TO FEEL AS THOUGH HE WAS TO BLAME FOR THAT AS WELL).*** *I love you, but I don't think this "thing" is going to manifest into anything permanent at this rate.  You know as much as I like the big things, little things*

     *The 1st Installment of the Kalico Jones Trilogy*

*mean just as much and it seems as though you have a problem with the little things. My holiday cards are late and I have to remind you on top of that. My birthday card read as though you were giving it to a co-worker, I don't know what to do at this point. I am not happy.*
*I hope we can be friends.*
*Sincerely,*
*k.j.*

I gave the letter to him over Buffalo wings and beer at Fridays. He took it pretty well. We debated over things such as the Birthday card and the sex thing, but for the most part, that was the beginning of the end of my association with Mr. Realtor.

We did go out several times after that and I did ask him for money, but we had a friendly understanding.

Translation: He would continue to assist me financially until I got on my feet.

Three months later, I was totally on my feet and he and I were no longer in contact.

Mr. Realtor, he's doing just fine. He calls me every year on my birthday.

I was starting to feel as though now would be a good time for me to cut everyone out of my life that meant me no good (Ebonics) and unfortunately that meant I had to cut off friends and several family members. Oh well, I can't let that bother me right now, 'cause based on the letters in my hand, I have to get my shit in order quick!

# TIME TO WAKE UP LITTLE GIRL THE WORLD IS WAITING

**What letters?**

The two letters I received in the mail this week, one informing of Mr. Diamond Bracelet's release from jail and the other letter was from Mr. Moore; he was transferred to NY and needed to see me right away.

Shit! How was I going to explain all this to my current boyfriend, Mr. Orgasm? He's been busy in the recording studio working on his solo project and so the times we do spend with each other are supposed to be GOOD times, right?

Wrong.

**Our conversation**

"What the fuck do you mean you have another man?"

"I never SAID that, what I am saying is, I have two friends both of whom need me right now and I have to be there for them."

"And so where does that leave me? Why would you spring this shit on me right in the middle of my project? You know I need you right now…what the fuck are you thinking?"

I walked toward Mr. Orgasm and put my arm on his shoulder, "It's not that I don't WANT to be with you, it's just that I CANNOT be your girlfriend, we can still be together, just not as much as we've been."

"Fuck you!"

He grabbed his jacket and stormed out of his own house. I collected my belongings and quietly left the premises.

# When Gucci Came First

He never did finish his solo project, damn.

In the meantime, I learned that the orgasm had nothing to do with why I was with him because he had nothing to do with the actual emotion behind it. I was emotional because I NEVER experienced that before and I wanted to so bad. But to be honest with you, when the feeling is over, it's over! Don't act like you don't agree, 'cause you know you understand.

Kicking people out of my life was easy, keeping them out of my life...now that was the hard part. It's been weeks since the last time I got high, but my drinking was still excessive. I told myself that I would rather be drunk than high. Only thing is when I got drunk, I started smoking cigarettes and next thing I knew, I would start to feel like I wanted to get high. I called my therapist, who I hadn't seen in a couple of weeks, I made an appointment.

# SESSION NO. 10 WITH THE THERAPIST

"Hello Kalico"
"Hello"
"How have you been?"
"Good and I haven't gotten high!"
"Well that's great Kalico."
"I still drink a lot, but the way I see it, drinking is better than being a coke head!"
"One accomplishment at a time, okay?'

I smiled. I was happy to see my therapist. I really was.

"Are you and your mom getting along?"

Okay, why is he going there? Couldn't he tell I was happy? I did not want to discuss my mother, especially since her and I were arguing last night over my lifestyle.

"No, we are not!"
"Do you want to talk about it?"
"No, I do not!"
"Okay"
"I have come to the conclusion that my mother and I have to try being friends instead of the traditional mother / daughter thing, 'because that's not working."
"I see"
"So please don't ask me anything about her, this is MY session."
"You're right. Well do you have something in particular you would like to talk about?"
"No"
"What made you stop getting high?"

"I didn't say I stopped getting high, I said that I HAVENT gotten high."

# When Gucci Came First

I could tell by the expression on my therapist's face, he was confused.  He was probably trying to figure out what in the hell was wrong with me, why I was being so difficult.

"Right"

We were silent for a while.

"Kalico"
"Yes"
"Is there something wrong?"
"I have a lot of things on my mind; you see I cut a lot of people out of my life over the past few weeks."
"Why?"
"I need to stand on my own two feet."
"Are you?"
"Yes, but it's difficult."
"But is it worth it?"
"Yeah, it's worth it."
"Have you made any travel arrangements lately?"
"To California?"
"Yes"
"Nah, I'm waiting 'til I finish my book."
"You're writing a book?"
"Yes"
"Why didn't you tell me?"
"My hobbies never came up."
"Well, that's great Kalico!"
"Yeah, I'm gonna be famous for the RIGHT reasons one day."
"I guess I'll see you on Oprah."
"I guess you will."

My fifty minutes were up, time to go.

I never went back to my therapist after that.  I wanted to heal myself.

Re-virginize myself.  That's what I was going to do. I was going to prove that a person could change their ways.  I was going to prove that just because you've done things you probably wish you hadn't, didn't mean you had to continue to do those things.  I was going to prove everybody wrong!  I stopped having sex and I widened my circle of friends and associations by going different places.  I began to get to know myself, by myself.  I took myself to the movies and out to dinner, the lengths of my skirts were longer, I now wanted to leave some things for people's imagination.  I stopped getting drunk to the point of memory loss and every time I saw someone from the "old Kalico" days, I said hello and kept going. I wasn't attracted to the junkie lifestyle anymore. My outlook on life had changed, I wanted something special out of life, and I wanted to live.

# IT'S MY BIRTHDAY OCTOBER 10TH

I promised myself that I would not continue to participate in things that made me unhappy.  It was time for me to finish cleaning myself emotionally.  I turned off my answering machine, cut off all the lights in my apartment and cried.  I had to get rid of the pain I was feeling.  I cried about misusing my body, I cried about all the beatings I got from my mother growing up, I cried about my drug abuse, I cried about being sexually abused by my baby sitter and his brothers, I cried because I felt my mother should have protected me from that, I cried because I was unhappy with the relationship I had with my father, I cried because I was unhappy with my job, I cried because my family was absent in my life, I cried because I was maturing, I cried because I was growing up, I cried because I was getting myself together, I cried because I was Kalico…FINALLY!

My goal was still the same, the only difference was my path.  I had actually begun to change my path in life.  It was scary, but it felt good.  I made a list of all the things I wanted to accomplish during this lifetime.  I shocked myself with what I wrote down:

I want a picture of all my sisters and brothers, nieces and nephews… together.

I couldn't get past that.  I couldn't think of anything else I wanted more than that picture and finishing this book.  I knew I wanted to work with teenage girls in some type of counseling capacity, but the most important thing to me was to one day be united with all my sisters and brothers AT THE SAME TIME!

Since my restoration, my family relations have been better.  My mother and I still have a love / hate relationship, but we are the best of friends.  Me, Joey and Charlie are closer than ever and we have a fantastic relationship with our father.  Extended family relations are still on the same, "see you at the next holiday dinner or funeral" basis, but we acknowledge the love when we do get together.

I still want to go to Los Angeles, and I plan to go very soon, but just for a visit.

I do not get high and I am not dating.

**Because I don't want to.**


**MY PRAYER...**

Precious Father, you have done so much to save me. You who are so holy and righteous have reached down to take my hand. Teach me your ways. Correct the wrongs in my life. Guide me into your truth. I want to not only be saved from my sin, but from days of uselessness and frustration. Make me a vessel that can be used to honor you. Through Jesus I pray, Amen.

Now, I am not going to tell you that I am HOLY now, but this is my prayer and I want to share it with you.  Just to give you something to hold on to from GOD and me.  That's it!

**"You should not suffer the past.  You should be able to wear it like a loose garment, take it off and let it drop."**
-Eva Jessye

Please go to www.amazon.com and www.barnesandnoble.com and write me a review!

# MY SINCERE THANKS...

Thank you God, I know my situation was "touch and go" for a while, but I'm still here, thanks to your GRACE and MERCY.  Thank you.

**To my Mother:** Who took care of three children who didn't understand how difficult it was raising three kids by herself,
**THANKS! To My Father:** Continue to do Gods work. **To My Brothers:** My heart splits in half, a piece for each of you. To Kimberly Hatwood: You are the strongest woman I have ever met, **TRUE STORY! Naomi – Hannunah Sabur** – I love and miss you. **Mike Moore:** This one's for you baby!  **Aunt Ethyl & Uncle Mike:** Thanks for the good times! **To Robert A Brown, Jr:** Thanks for being a great friend. **To ENTIRE Money Earnin' Mt. Vernon, "What's Up?" The entire Y.O. – Yonkers, I love y'all – School Street, Riverdale, Whitney Young, Warburton, Lawrence, Bruce...Thanks for the memories.  To the members of The Kalico Jones Project and Authors Helping Authors at Yahoo groups:** Thanks 4 da luv!

**STRAIGHT UP ...NO CHASER "Where my dogs at":**
G-Money (Washington, DC), J.M. Benjamin (Author), Brother Pete (J.M's Brother...I love you), Brandon (East Orange, NJ), Boo & Entire 3-D Barbershop (Montclair, NJ), Pete Clark (Mt. Vernon, NY), Red Dred (Miss you man), Chalah (Mt. Vernon, NY), Q.L. (Miss you too), Boobie, Trouble, LuLu, Kdub, Reggie Barnes, Q Bomber (RIP), Chaka, Shameka, Juanita, Azizi, Carolyn (We'll talk again one day), Aaron Duncan, Kenya Renee, Darlene & Charlene, and if I am forgetting anyone, trust me its not on purpose. Oh and my Uncle Butter – Can't forget him (Mt. Vernon, NY) GHP FOREVER!!! GOTTI, Cool T and the Brothers (Yonkers, NY), Black Ass Inky (hahaha, You know I love you and your mom), Mr. M3 BMW who folks said died of AIDS and he did, but did you know he had a blood transfusion when he had a motorcycle accident? Yep, so let's put that shit about him to the side and move on. Mt. Vernon, NY – AIDS/HIV is nothing to joke about or spread rumors about. If you know someone who has it, let THEM tell it. Stop it with the rumors; it's not right...please. Supreme = Preemie (I

love you and I'm proud of you), and all my MySpace friends: Cotton Candy, Sweet Cooch Brown (and the rest of the Brooklyn Bombshells, I love these young ladies), Yo Nitty – Harlem, don't ask why…that's my homie. Ant Live 129 another homie…Tawana, LALA, **and last but most certainly FAR from least, MY BOO and Sister…Tiph Jackson. I love you. And me and you…we rock like Ike and Tina sometimes, but we're THICK as thieves and we don't apologize. Tiph, You are forever my people. FOREVER my sister.** More to go: Q = Brown Eyes…Mt. Vernon is known for having some of the Prettiest Black Men in the world. I love you all! I know I'm forgetting folks but again, it's not on purpose. Buddy, Tootie =RIP, Reggie Patrick, Travis, Worm, Matt Terry (of whom has yet to pick up the dog I brought for him- hahaha) and just everyone who loves me for who I am. Minus this Kalico Jones Shhhhhhhh! Muah!

**Now before my bloodline starts coming for me. I love you all. All my brothers and sisters and there are a ton of us. But I will just sound off like this:** Lisa, NuNu, Valencia, Shantel, Tykeshia, Danasia, Tremell, Travon, Tyree, Josh and Andre, Joey and Charlie  - WHEW…Daddy please no more! I hope I didn't forget any of you and misspell your names too bad. Next book, I'll get the names right! I love you all and I love all of your children and in Lisa's case…GRAND children.

**To Stacia & Cathy Duke:**
What can I say? I love you both and I don't know if you know just how much your kind words meant to me. During that "time" in my life, I just couldn't see my way through. I thank you both and HARVEY! Muah. I love you!

SLEEP "HOLD YA HEAD!!!!" (HARLEM)
WHATS UP WITH ME?
Write Kalico: kalicojones@yahoo.com
www.myspace.com/kalico_jones
WWW.THEKALICOJONESPROJECT.COM

*And now for your sneak peek into book two…*

# REFLECTIONS

I must admit my current circumstance is largely due to my inability to
let go of a useless situation.
My inability to cut the cord
when it comes to holding on to hope.
Hope for what?
Hope for something that may never be
Something for my daughter

...A father

Don't ever let it be too late for you!


**TWO YEARS AFTER BOOK ONE ENDS:**

**Prelude to a revelation...**
I can't believe I'm stuck here, in the house, with a baby, while HIS ass is out
running the streets.  I have no money, no food and I'm all the way in Spring
Valley.

I called my friend Monet.  She left her job and came right over, handed me
$100.00 (of which I haven't paid her back to this date) and proceeded to
give me the advice every woman in my situation gets from that one girlfriend,
who even though you are down in the dumps feels she has to give you in
order to **KEEP IT REAL...**
"Girl you need to leave his ass!"

"This shit is crazy, in the house with a newborn and no money, he can't be
serious!" she continued... "Where's the food? Where's the pampers?"

That's when it HIT me, my ass needed to put together that FUCK YOU
money quick.  I had to not only exit, but also exit with a kid. Where did this

go wrong?

I checked the time, it was 1 O'clock in the afternoon, is he okay? And if he is okay, where is he?

The phone rang.

Ring...ring...
"Hello" (it was a Famous R&B Singer)

"Yo what up Kalico, yo "Wiz" (short for Wisdom), just left my house, he's on his way home, aight?"

I said okay and hung up the phone. I was on fire. How DARE Mr. Famous R&B Singer call my house to tell me that MY MAN was on his way home at 1 O'clock in the afternoon.

Where in the hell was he all night?  I put the baby in her crib and waited for him to open the door.  It's now 2:30pm and homeboy is just walking in the house!  He's drunk and shit...looking pitiful, talking about, "I know...I know...I fucked up, I'm sorry...you mad?"

I took a deep breath, no this nigga did not just ask me if I was mad, he must have bumped his fucking head on the way upstairs.  I closed my eyes and thought to myself...I should slap his ass but he's so drunk he probably wouldn't feel it.  I will be calm...I will not hit him...I will just leave...I will be calm...I will not hit him...I will just leave...I will be calm...I will not hit him...I will just leave.

I looked at him and in a damn near whisper said, "Yes, I am mad, I'm furious, you're a father now, we are a family, this is crazy...I'm leaving!"
**Two weeks later...I was gone!**

# BOOK TWO: COMING SOON!
# "AND TO YOU HOMEBOY I SAY THANKS"

(when what doesn't kill you makes you stronger)

# When Gucci Came First

**KJ THREE SIX FIVE (The Diary Vol. 1)**

Daily entries taken directly from my site and published, at the advice of my readers.

**08/19 - Hello all...today's reflections are a product of family circumstances.** I mention the truth shall set you free...so I will say this: What good is keeping "the peace" when the peace is phony? It's your place to demand respect from others and family is no exception. When difficulties arise, get your point across and don't waive your feelings for the sake of keeping peace. You'll only harbor resentment. **-kJ**

**08/31 -Or what I like to call, "The Final Day of Summer"** School shopping, looking for a new place to live - possibly a relocation, and completing my second book. I'm tired, I've got some things going on and I just deleted myself from the long list of Authors groups I belonged to. No reason to explain, just I feel at this time I do not need to be part of a clique to advance in publishing. I feel as though the streets are my reviewers, so no thanks on that. I'm not trying to be funny, I don't think I'm better than others...but let's face it. I'm FROM the streets and so that's who I let judge me. Kalico send us 9 copies of your book for review? NO. Kalico we would like to add you to our web page, just let us review your book, and by the way...we need 4 copies. NO thanks. I will continue to let the streets handle my book sales, and reviews, your help is not necessary at this time. Publishing to me is a business! I'm not here to make friends with everyone who comes across my path. I'm just here to make a difference. I'm sure you can understand that.

# When Gucci Came First

So today I say, Blaze your OWN trail. Be your OWN judge and don't let anyone dictate your life to you! peace! KJ.

**09/01- Today's topic. When enough is ENOUGH!**
You have friends, you have family, and you have associates, all out for one thing, Your time. But when do you begin to put a dollar amount = value on YOUR time? When does your time become valuable to you? I have come to the conclusion - just for today, of course - that my time is VALUABLE and therefore should not be wasted. Don't waste my time. You need something, ask, get it and move on. Don't expect me to babysit you. don't expect me to allow you to reach your goals via my time. I've got my own goals. So any time I take out for you is time taken away from me. So please if someone is nice enough to help you, learn whatever it is they are doing for you, so you can do it for yourself. Don't be a time waster. - **KJ.**

**09/03-Well today I will be traveling, actually for the next week I am traveling.** Going South. Maybe find a home for my family and me. Check out the book stores in the area, been getting a lot of country love re: When Gucci Came First, so you know a sista gots to go around and check in on those who have supported me. Introduce them to the new books - that's right, BOOKS, plural and just relax. Tried to have a conversation with baby daddy this morning, too bad it didn't go as planned. Ok see this is why ladies WE have got to do "it" for ourselves. WE have to be independent of the b.s. Life is better for you when you treat baby daddy like a business transaction. Damn shame I have to say this, but you know your girl Kal, she's gonna be real...If he ain't going to give your child the love and respect and most Important, TIME...then make sure your child gets the money. **Don't try to force him to do what he should feel in his heart. Always keeping it real, KJ over and OUT!**

**9/13 - The day after the weekend it stormed...** I can't even tell you guys how this weekend has made me stop and think, "When did Kalico become a punk?" First, my car was Impounded, yes, Impounded and I was given five tickets two of them court appearances, then I had drama with baby daddy You see, unfortunate for him, he didn't enlist what I like to call, **CONSEQUENTIAL THINKING.** It's when you think about the consequences of your actions frame by frame prior to acting on dumb ass Impulses. You have to evaluate how your irrational behavior is going to affect the overall relationships (you and your children, you and the mother of your child, you and the relatives of the mother of your child, your children's relationships with your family, etc). All these things should be taken into consideration, because when they are, you usually don't show your ass. Today is eviction day for those people who have taken up too much of my mental and emotional time. Eviction day for those individuals who feel as though they are going to affect my life in ways that force me to act out of character... to you, the space holders..."YOUR LEASE IS UP!" The flip side to this is they're all going to make me rich in the long run. **So on this day, Monday September 13, I say to my former tenants "Thank you...now pack your shit and go!" Keeping it real as always, your girl Kal**

**09/14 - The day after the day after the weekend it stormed... and I think I'm going to move.** Relocation may just help me sort the givers from the takers and provide the space between us I need to be able to get things in order. Just because you're an author, of which I do not consider myself to be because my books are truth based and not "made up" (to those who read the original When Gucci Came First: true tales of a tramp). So as I was saying, just because you're an author does mean you're Immune to daily drama and believe me ... I've got my share. Although it has been quiet today. Thank Goodness...**Love you all -KJ over and OUT!**

 Today I want to talk about haters in the "writing community" why? Authors don't hate on me because I'm trying to do my thing. Don't hate on me because I deleted myself from all of your groups, don't be mad because it APPEARS that I may be selling a book or two...I say this after seeing a post re: my book. Now for all y'all who know me you know I'm going to keep it real...this post was classless. called my book INANE PRATTLE, etc. Now that would have offended me HAD I NOT been selling books, that may have offended me HAD I NOT been doing my thing on so many OTHER levels, but fortunate for ME, I AM NOT a hater. I don't have to diss any of you authors, and why should I? and why would I? I've got all y'all books! I have support many of my peers, many authors' books are in my home and I DIDNT GET THEM FOR FREE! The ONLY book I have that I didn't pay for is by someone named Natalie, all the others...RIGHT OUT OF MY POCKET. I was the ONLY author out at the Harlem Book Fair giving out my books for FREE! I was the only author who can honestly say they went around and showed loved to EVERYONE! And in the midst of me being KJ...Not one of them said, "Oh let me buy a book from you kj." But did that stop my flow? Hell no. Did that make me not want to support you? Hell no! So why diss me? If I don't want to send books to be reviewed, don't take it personal, **I TOLD Y'ALL I WAS WRITING, LIVING AND DREAMING FOR THE STREETS, it's NOT personal. Kalico Jones is a MOVEMENT, WHERE STREET CREDIBILITY MEETS CORPORATE THINKING. I AM**

THE BRICK LAYER FOR ALLTHOSE LITTLE KIDS COMING UP WHO ARE IN SITUATIONS WHERE THEY FEEL AS THOUGH THEY CANNOT TURN TO ANYONE. I do many charitable events, I give my time, my money and my spirit for the kids, and don't you even THINK FOR ONE MINUTE YOU CAN JUDGE ME! Please. Now I have better things to do for others, and I can't get them done by allowing the B.S. to get in the way of my goals. Y'all be cool out there. KJ over and OUT! Peace

09/27 - The REAL meaning of keeping it real...and today I'm forced to axe yet another person out of my life. But don't cry for me though, its all good. Now let's get to what I've been up to, my daughter being in a fashion show, dance class, karate, a festival, shopping, dinner, etc. and its been non-stop since Friday afternoon. I've been all over with an authors meeting, a book club meeting and just being a mommy. So between my little princess and my own stuff, it's been one heck of a couple of days. Her fashion debut... well you know how that went down...SHE DID HER THING! she was cute and professional, let me tell you, I may be grooming the next T. Banks. And the dance class, she was terrific! Did you expect anything less than perfection? Of course not! lol. I'm a proud mom. And I should be., it's really all good and I can look and say, **"this is because of me" and God has my back and YOURS too! See ya when I see ya...Kali**

*The Final Installment of the Kalico Jones Trilogy*

# 4 MILES TO FREEDOM
# COMING SOON

Yelling in the background…
"Tell Kalico not to call here again, we don't want to get involved, whatever is going on between her and homeboy is none of our business, hang up on her ass right now Rich!"

I was on the phone with one of homeboy's cousins, asking him for a number. During our talk, I told him how homeboy hadn't seen his daughter in over one year and was behind in child support. I was only calling to ask for his assistance…to help me help my daughter. We had been in and out of emergency rooms due to what was thought to be Sickle Cell, the doctors needed homeboy's medical history.

I didn't know who else to turn to.

I could not believe Rich's wife, girlfriend or whatever she goes by these days after having just had her third kid by this, another looser in the family…she was yelling, cursing and did she call me a bitch?
Ha…that was easy for her to do, as I was in New Jersey and her ass was in Mt. Vernon. Yeah, I will be that bitch, and maybe homeboy is a looser, but for the most part and other than that…WE – me and my daughter are just fine.

"Richard, why is Adrianne yelling like that in the background? What did I do to her?" as I was utterly confused by her behavior.

"KJ, she does not want you to call here any more. We all know homeboy is fucking up, but there is nothing we can do about it. That's for you two to work out."
"Are you serious? So you're not going to give me his telephone number?"
"No"
"But its Sickle Cell Richard…( took a deep breath) can you please get in contact with him and just give him the number to the hospital? Please?"

# When Gucci Came First

(more yelling in the background by Adrianne) "Tell her no…we are not getting involved! I told you to hang up!"

I pleaded with Richard to please just pass along the number to homeboy, and as soon as he agreed, his "whatever" got on the phone and said, "Take care of your own business bitch!" and hung up.

WOW, can you believe that shit? This ingrate just hung up on me. She has three children, so it's hard for me to digest the fact that as a mother herself, she showed no compassion for my daughter. Wow.

I called back and let the phone ring. No one picked up.
Good. I will just leave a voice message.

"Hello this is KJ, my apologies for impeding upon your privacy with my issue, clearly this is something that does not involve you, but there is a child in the hospital and this is urgent. I just need to contact homeboy. The doctors are requesting blood work and a possible bone marrow sample from him. They are in need of his family's medical history. We are at Mountainside Hospital in Montclair, NJ should you wish to pass along this message." I left the telephone number to the hospital, my cell number, my job number and my mother's information as well…

I deleted Speedy's cell phone number after that.

NO ONE got back to us.

NO ONE called the hospital.

I even called homeboy's job.

And …
NOTHING.
Eighteen tests for all sorts of shit and six days later, my daughter was released from the hospital with a clean bill of health.

Thank GOD.
And still not a peep from homeboy.
Notice how I do not capitalize his name. There is no respect there and so I refuse to do it. So don't worry yourself with that…Just wanted to get that out of the way in the beginning. At any rate, life goes on.

# Who is MiMi Williamson aka Kalico Jones?

*Mimi Williamson* is the founder of *The Kalico Jones Project (an online business networking group for African Americans)* and Sole Proprietor of *WildChild Press,* an independent publishing resource for authors who wish to self-publish their works.

She is a resident of East Orange, New Jersey by way of Mt. Vernon, NY where she continues to lend her support. In 2007, *Mimi Williamson* assisted her hometown with it's Mayoral campaign by hosting several online radio interviews with current Mayor Mr. Clinton Young and former Mayor Mr. Ernest Davis, which was one of the closest Mayoral races in Mt. Vernon history, and by far the most controversial.

Her grass roots approach to rally young voters was recognized and applauded by both current Mayor Mr. Clinton Young and former Mayor Mr. Ernest Davis.

As a young lady who grew up in an environment that was abusive. *Mimi Williamson,* made a conscious decision to not only pen her life story under the brand, *"Kalico Jones"* but to actively work to assist young people in their quest to become successes in their own right. She prides herself on her determination to "Beat the odds" by focusing on her education and natural talents.

Although her titles (five books and counting…) are not for audiences under 18, *Mimi Williamson's* life experiences give her added value at what she does. Physically abused, sexually abused, emotionally abused, drugs, being kicked out of school at 16, *Mimi Williamson* appeared to be a statistic.

But despite being told she would never amount to anything, *Mimi Williamson* turned her life around. She set realistic goals for herself and achieved them one by one. At 19 she graduated from Monroe College in New Rochelle, NY and by the time she was 21, she was working at a leading Wall Street firm. She then went on to secure positions within National Geographic Magazine, Deloitte & Touché and WorldCom, all leading companies in their respective fields at the time.

During her "time" in Corporate America, *Mimi Williamson* realized her true passion; to work with "at risk" teens and women / families in transitional stages, and so I introduce to you…*Mimi Williamson* AND *The Kalico Jones project.*

***COMMUNITY INITIATIVES UNDER THE KJP:***

## CROSS OUR T'S

Cross Our Ts was created by Mimi Williamson, who has taken a personal interest in promoting the importance of education, self respect, and health & well being to teens, including HIV/AIDS prevention, through interactive teen friendly seminars.

*"Cross Our T's offers teens REAL life solutions in an open dialogue to REAL life issues and concerns."*

## KJ CARES

A community based organization that believes in grassroots approaches to community challenges. Fund Raising initiatives. Voter registration drives. Food / Clothing drives. A true effort to immobilize the surrounding community leaders / business owners, residents to GIVE BACK!

## The KALICO JONES Project

*Black2Black* Business Networking

Mission: To provide a networking resource that expands the possibilities of initial ideas, and concepts according to the "each one teach one" methodology for the African American Community.

*"By sharing information we allow our efforts to be supported and developed through the experiences and assistance of others."*

## KJ's KIDS

For Kids, about Kids, KJ loves the kids!

Events / Book Clubs / Scholarships and more!

For speaking engagements please call 973-672-2753

Email: kalicojones@yahoo.com

Website: www.thekalicojonesproject.com

# When Gucci Came First

*"The Cross Our T's" initiative & The Kalico Jones Project is a wonderful program headed by a person who in all rights is a hero herself."*

www.ingramcontent.com/pod-product-compliance
Lightning Source LLC
Chambersburg PA
CBHW020328110726
47898CB00003B/792